Discover
fresh
fiction

to entice every reader

Multnomah Publishers® *Sisters, Oregon*

Let's Talk Fiction © 2003

Multnomah Publishers, Inc.

High Stakes © 2003

by Kathy Herman

Sisterchicks on the Loose © 2003

by Robin's Ink, LLC

Steal Away © 2003

by Linda Hall

The Lights of Tenth Street © 2003

by Veritas Enterprises, Inc.

The Breaking Point © 2003

by Karen Ball

Autumn Dreams © 2003

by Gayle G. Roper

Antonia's Choice © 2003

by Nancy Rue

All My Tomorrows © 2003

by ALJO Productions

A Steadfast Surrender © 2003

by Nancy Moser

Sold Out © 2003

by Melody Carlson

For information:
MULTNOMAH PUBLISHERS, INC.
POST OFFICE BOX 1720
SISTERS, OREGON 97759

Dear Readers:

We are thrilled to present you with this sampling of inspirational novels. Within these pages you will find a glimpse into ten new captivating fiction titles filled with adventure, mystery, humor, faith, love, and romance.

For a limited time these books are on sale at your local Christian bookstore. We encourage you to pick up your copies today.

In His love and grace,

Sandy Muller
Fiction Marketing Manager
Multnomah Publishers
www.letstalkfiction.com

High Stakes

by Kathy Herman, The Baxter series, Book Four
ISBN 1-59052-081-5, U.S. Suggested Retail Price: $11.99
320 pages, trade paperback, Fiction/General/Suspense

Available Now

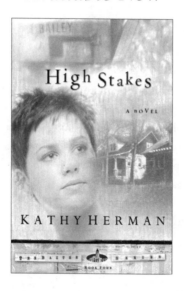

Angie Marks, pierced and tattooed, arrives on
Baxter's door-step and wanders homeless until an
eccentric old millionaire shocks everyone and hires
her to be his live-in housekeeper. Down at Monty's
Diner, the rumor mill goes on full tilt, and suspicion
abounds that Angie might be in cahoots with Billy
Joe Sawyer to frighten key witnesses in his upcom-
ing conspiracy/murder trial.

But events here take a sharp right turn. Hang

on! A *lot* more is at stake than Angie's reputation! She finds herself implicated in a grisly murder and then is forced into hiding by the man accused of the crime. This fourth book in the Baxter series is full of twists and turns that will keep you guessing until the end.

I wrote *High Stakes* to be more than edge-of-your-seat suspense...it's a touching story of a troubled young woman and a determined old man who refuses to give up on her. It digs deeply into the human yearning for love and acceptance. And it poignantly reminds us how foolish it is to judge a person by outward appearance.

This story is my favorite in the Baxter series. The characters are forever etched on my heart.

Kathy Herman

Sample Chapter

Angie Marks looked out the window of Tully Hollister's blue Ford pickup and bemoaned the sagging gray sky that had followed her from Memphis. She was only vaguely aware of the driver's incessant talking until the car in front of them hit a puddle and a gush of water flooded the windshield.

"At least it stopped rainin'," Tully said. "Last I heard we got over four inches... You awake?"

"Uh-huh."

"Not much for talkin', are you?"

Angie stared out the window. *Like I could get a word in.*

"Know anything about herpetology?" Tully asked.

Angie shook her head. "What is it?"

"The study of reptiles."

"Guess I missed out on that one." His boring babble annoyed her more than the wipers scraping the dry windshield.

"I'm fascinated by reptiles," Tully said. "Especially snakes."

"Not like that guy on TV, I hope."

"Yep. I pick 'em up with my bare hands. Take all kinds of chances."

He looked at her as if waiting for a reaction. Angie avoided his eyes, wishing he'd keep them on the road.

"I caught a whole mess of rattlesnakes," he said. "Picked up every one of 'em without gettin' bit."

"Lucky you."

"Now they're in a gunnysack in my shed. Wanna know why?"

She didn't.

"Because they're dangerous. I'm attracted to *wild* things." He looked at her and grinned.

Was that supposed to be a pass? Angie cringed. "How much farther is it?"

"Not far. Why didn't you take the bus? Bet your folks wouldn't like the idea of you hitchhikin'."

"My connection didn't leave till ten o'clock. I didn't wanna get in after dark."

"Lucky for you I came along when I did or you'd be soppin' wet."

"Yeah, I know. Thanks." Angie sat as close as she could to the passenger door, glad that her backpack was between them.

"Where'd you say you were from?" Tully asked.

"Memphis."

"Baxter isn't exactly on the way to anything. You visitin' relatives?"

Angie shook her head.

"Nothin' else to do there."

"I followed the news story about the virus and the fire bombings last summer. Thought maybe I could meet the father who saved his twin sons."

"Dennis Lawton?"

Angie nodded. "You know him?"

"Shoot, yes. Everybody knows Lawton. Rich outsider from Denver. Moved here to be closer to his boys. Finally married their mother last weekend."

"Really? He married Jennifer Wilson?"

"Had some fancy-schmancy weddin' at that church downtown and then a big wingding out at the country club. Everyone was talkin' about it."

"Did his family come for the wedding?" Angie asked.

"Beats me. His grandfather lives here now. Why you askin'?"

"Just curious."

He grinned, his eyes seeming to probe. "What're you after, girl?"

Angie looked out the window again, glad to see the sun peeking out of the dark clouds. "People in Baxter seem real nice from what I saw on TV—different from the people I'm used to. Seems like a friendly town."

"Yep, it's friendly all right. But I gotta tell you, that silver thing on your nose and those tattoos aren't gonna set well with folks around here."

Angie pulled her jacket up over her shoulders.

"Whoa, a double rainbow!" Tully pointed out her window. "Must be a sign I'm gonna win at poker tonight. You know much about poker?"

Angie sighed and glanced at her watch. "Are we getting close?"

"There's the courthouse," Tully said. "See the clock tower sticking up through those trees?"

Angie leaned forward in the seat. From the top of the hill, she saw a town nestled below. "That's Baxter? I'm really here?"

"Yep. Where do you want me to drop you off?"

"How about the town square?" Angie looked at the cottage-style houses and the wide streets overhung with shade trees. The grass seemed so green. As they rode down Baxter Avenue, she marveled at the dogwood trees and all the colorful flowers. The town was even prettier than she thought it would be.

"You act like you never seen trees before," Tully said.

Angie felt herself blushing.

A few seconds later, he pulled into a parking space in front of the courthouse. "There you go."

Angie sat for a moment, her eyes fixed on the Baxter icon she had seen so many times on the news.

"Where're you stayin'?" Tully asked. "That break in the clouds won't last. Gonna be dark pretty soon."

"Uh, I haven't decided yet. Thanks for the lift." Angie scooted out of the truck, grabbed her backpack, then looked over at Tully. "Any idea where Dennis Lawton lives?"

"Built quite a place out on CR 632. Want me to take you there?"

"No. Just curious."

"You know what they say about curiosity…" He flashed a toothy grin. "Watch your step, *Nine Lives.*"

Angie shut the door. As Tully backed out and drove away, her eyes surveyed the grounds around the courthouse. City Park looked the same as it had on TV.

She put on her leather jacket, then slipped on her backpack and strolled once around the square, stopping in front of the courthouse as the clock tower chimed seven. A raindrop landed on her head. Then another on her sleeve. She put her hands in her pockets and felt the bus ticket stub.

It had cost her everything she had to get here. What if it backfired?

At Monty's Diner, a loud clap of thunder caused the lights to flicker as rain rolled in sheets down the east wall of windows. The early crowd sat elbow-to-elbow at the counter and lingered over Saturday's edition of the *Baxter Daily News.*

"Well, here we go," said Assistant Manager Mark Steele. "The jury selection has started for Sawyer's trial."

"That no-good better get life after the havoc he wreaked in this town," George Gentry said.

Rosie Harris picked up a Denver omelette and slid it in front of George. "You worried the jury will go easy on him?"

"Only in Afghanistan." George smiled and held up his cup for a refill.

Mark sighed. "Let's talk about something else."

"Well," Rosie put her hand on her hip, "I heard the star witness is back from his honeymoon."

"The Lawtons are home?" Mark said.

Rosie looked at Hattie Gentry and winked. "You don't suppose the newlyweds have other things to think about besides the trial?"

"After what Sawyer put those kids through," Hattie said, "they deserve a little happiness."

Rosie nodded. "It's wonderful they're finally a family. That Dennis is movie-star gorgeous. What a catch for Jennifer: Mrs. Dennis Christopher Lawton…has a nice ring to it."

"So does her left hand," George said. "Bet that cost him a wad."

"And did you check out the Mercedes SUV he bought her?" Mark said. "Wanna bet her pain and suffering got up and went?"

"Yeah, there's just something healing about the color green, especially in neat little stacks." George winked at Mark.

Rosie shook her head. "You guys are hopeless."

"Aw, that whippersnapper Lawton's probably into somethin' shady," Mort Clary said.

George rolled up the newspaper and bopped Mort lightly on the head. "For once, can't you just let things *be?*"

"Well, Georgie, the boy don't work. Has money comin' out his ears. Where do ya suppose he gits it all?"

"Ever occur to you he might be independently wealthy?" Mark said. "I heard his grandfather gave him money."

Mort wrinkled his nose. "That Patrick Bailey fella who moved here from Denver? I got no reason to trust him. Could be launderin' his stash and livin' simple like the rest of us to avoid suspicion."

Mark burst into laughter. "Yeah, Mort, maybe Mr. Bailey's in cahoots with the upper echelon of the Brownie Scouts…and moved to our strategic location to launder massive profits from cookie sales. Give me a break!"

"Laugh all ya want, Mr. High-and-Mighty Assistant Manager, but there's lotsa money comin' from somewhere. In my book, a fella oughta earn it outright."

"Oh, pleeease," Rosie said. "Can't we just be excited that those adorable twin boys finally have their parents together and they're all going to live happily ever after? Baxter could use a little pixie dust after what Sawyer and the Citizen's Watch Dogs did to this town."

George folded his newspaper and laid it aside. "I'm happy for the Lawtons. But I don't envy Dennis having to testify. Why, this thing could drag on for years."

On Saturday afternoon, Angie Marks sat in City Park, her legs drawn up, her back resting against a budding oak tree. The grass underneath her was damper than the muggy April breeze. She'd been there for two hours, and no one had spoken to her, though she had managed to evoke a few cautious smiles.

Angie was amused that most adults pretended not to see her. The children all stared and were hurried along by parents who probably assumed she was up to no good. Her cropped, black hair and pale skin accentuated the rows of pierced earrings and a silver stud above one nostril. But flower tattoos on her upper arms and around her wrists cinched the effect she was looking for. More body art was hidden underneath the black jeans and black tank top. The only thing remotely conventional about her was the pair of Birkenstocks into which her feet had willingly conformed.

Angie looked up and saw a small boy racing toward her, chasing a runaway soccer ball that hit the tree and bounced into her lap. She smiled and tossed the ball back to the child. The boy's mother marched up behind him, grabbed the ball from his hands as if Angie had contaminated it, and dragged her son away without bothering to say thank you.

Angie expected people to be turned off by the way she looked. Big deal. At least when she could control the reason why people were mean to her, it didn't hurt so much.

All she had going for her was the fifty dollars she took from her stepfather's wallet, a backpack containing two changes of clothes, and the hope she could find a job working near Heron Lake where the tourist season would soon be in full swing.

Her focus shifted to a striking couple pushing a double stroller with identical twins. The babies each had a head full of blond curls. Their eyes were wide and their expressions animated as they bounced in the stroller, babbling in stereo at a floppy-eared puppy that yelped and romped alongside.

The mother of the twins saw her and looked the other way. But their father's eyes connected with Angie's until her heart started to race and she looked down at her hands.

The couple passed by her, and when they had gone a short distance down the sidewalk, the husband looked back and caught Angie's eye a second time. His wife nudged him with her elbow, and the man turned around and kept walking.

Angie couldn't take her eyes off him as they walked away. Everything fit. That had to be him!

Sisterchicks on the Loose

by Robin Jones Gunn, a sisterchick™ novel
·ISBN 1-59052-198-6, U.S. Suggested Retail Price: $12.99
325 pages, trade paperback, Fiction/General/Contemporary
Reader's Group Discussion Questions Available

May 2003

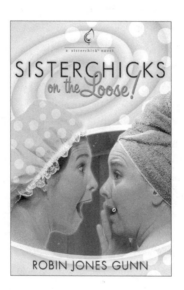

Zany antics abound when best friends Sharon and
Penny take off on a midlife adventure to Finland,
returning home with a new view of God and a new
zest for life.

Over the years I've received many letters from readers who said what they loved most about the Glenbrooke series was watching the friendships develop between the women characters. One reader told me, "I felt as if I was right there with the Glenbrooke women as I read about them sharing their hearts and lives with each other. I wanted my friendships to be that close. Your novels motivated me to enter a deeper level of honesty and caring with my dearest friends, and as that happened, I was amazed at how God changed our lives."

That's when the idea for *sisterchicks* was hatched!

For a long time I'd been thinking about writing novels about best friends. I wanted to take readers to a place they'd never been and let them feel as if they made some new friends along the way. For this first sisterchick novel, the story had been floating on the surface of my imagination for a long time. I wanted to loosely base the story on an adventure I took to Finland with my best friend years ago. What an experience! We laughed long, prayed hard, discovered some incredible chocolate, and came home changed.

Sisterchicks are everywhere. Maybe you have a few in your life already and didn't realize it. My sweetest hope is that you connect with such a woman or two on your life journey and find your joys doubled and your burdens cut in half.

If you get a chance, I'd love for you to come by for a visit at www.sisterchicks.com.

Robin Jones Gunn

SAMPLE CHAPTER

The plane had taken off while Penny and I were in the midst of our discussion. Penny opened her mouth wide and rubbed behind her left ear. I felt compelled to do the same, even though my ears weren't popping.

Penny continued to talk about the love notes she had worked on all night. She described how surprised she felt over her last-minute reluctance to leave her family. "I didn't expect to feel this way. And you know what, Sharon? I have to apologize for a couple of things. First, I want to apologize for being so cold when you were going through the trauma with Ben. I didn't understand. I think I do now. Sorry I wasn't more sympathetic."

"It's okay. I needed to hear what you said. You were right. I'm glad I didn't back out of the trip."

"Really?" Penny's left eyebrow went up.

"Yes, really. Why do you ask? What's the surprise?"

"Is my eyebrow up?"

"Yes."

"Rats! I'm going to have to work on that. I do have another little surprise, and I think you're going to need to read all my facial quirks when I tell you this."

I looked hard at her. I'd forgotten how intense Penny's gaze could be. She had a way of seeing into people as if she were shining a light so the person could search for something lost along the way. I don't know why I let her do that to me. I could turn away and listen sufficiently without looking. But I didn't. I allowed her dark eyes to shine their amber-flecked light on me because Penny knew things. She saw things way before I did. Right now she was looking for something.

Apparently I had it.

"This is the other thing I was going to apologize to you about. We don't exactly have everything lined up in Finland. Which I think is fine because all our options are open. But I didn't want you to feel—" Penny searched for the right word—"uncomfortable."

"That's okay. What needs to be worked on? I have the tour book. We could do some planning now."

"Yes," Penny said slowly.

"What about your aunt? Did she give you any specifics in her letter about things to do?"

Penny's finger went up to her lips. "No. You see, I never heard back from my aunt. And before you say anything, Sharon, it's not that big a deal. We have plenty of money. We can stay at any hotel we want the whole time, if we need to. I wasn't necessarily planning to stay at my aunt's house. I just wanted to meet her. But I don't even know if she's still alive. It's not that important, though. We can try to track her down once we arrive. But if we don't find her, we'll just have fun exploring."

I didn't say anything right away. I'm certain both my eyebrows were down. Penny was watching me carefully.

"So, you're telling me that we got on this plane and we're flying halfway across the world, but when we arrive, we don't have any idea what we'll do."

"Yes and no. We'll take a taxi and find a hotel. Or rent a car. And we'll find a restaurant and have some dinner. Or lunch, or whatever mealtime it will be then. And," she added on an upbeat note, "we'll pray and see what God puts in our path."

I wanted to scold her. I wanted to say, "Penny, people like us don't just show up in big foreign cities in the middle of winter and start looking up names of reputable hotels in a phone book!"

Before I could speak, Penny said, "I know I should have said something earlier, but I kept thinking I'd hear from my aunt at the last minute. I brought all the information I have about her with me. We'll take each step, each day as it comes. Like I said, we've got plenty of money." Penny's eyes were ablaze with dancing sprinkles of hope. "Whatever happens, I know it will be an adventure."

I reminded myself that "adventure" had been Penny's objective all along, even in the church nursery so long ago. And I had told Jeff I didn't want old age to be the only risky trip I ever took. This was it.

Risky. Adventuresome. Ridiculous.

At this moment, the appropriate adjective didn't matter because when a person is thirty thousand feet in the air, seat belted in business class, she is, for all practical purposes, committed. Two months ago I never would have dreamed up any of this. Two days ago I was still trying to work up the courage to board that plane in Portland by myself. Two minutes ago, however, Penny's left eyebrow went up, and secretly I wanted it to. I wanted Penny to surprise me and make me uncomfortable.

"What do you say, Sharon?" Penny looked at me hard. "Are you okay with this? I know you like life to be organized, but the thing is, now we'll be completely at God's mercy, and nothing is more adventuresome than that!"

With a deep breath, I gave my dearest friend the gift she had always so freely given me, the gift she was looking for when she looked so deeply into my eyes. I gave her grace. "Sure. I'm fine with this. We'll figure it out as we go along."

"Perfect! I was hoping you wouldn't be mad. This is going

to be great; you'll see. We're going to have the kind of trip they never write about in the tour books."

My better sense told me I should mention people had good reasons for not abandoning themselves haphazardly to God's mercy, and such erratic trips weren't written about in the tour books for good reasons. But I pressed my lips together and enjoyed the sensation of once again being in the wake of the fabulous, fearless, flying Penny.

Penny and I went through the tour book, circling potential hotels and finding a phone number for a taxi company. Until we arrived, we couldn't do much more.

I bent down to put away the tour book, and something extraordinary happened. The clouds, which had cushioned our flight for the past few hours, cleared, and a burst of sunshine spilled in through the window. I turned to lower the window shade and found myself staring *down* on snow-covered mountains. They looked like a row of little girls dressed for their first Holy Communion. They seemed to be waiting for their cue to begin the processional march. I'd never seen anything so pure and majestic.

"Penny, look."

She leaned over. "I wonder if those are the Canadian Rockies. Or would we be past them by now? We're traveling north, aren't we? Into the sun. Our winter day will be short. Canada is so beautiful."

Penny flitted through a recounting of a story I'd heard many times. I guessed it to be one of her favorite memories since she told it often. Two summers before we met, Penny and Dave rode his Harley from California to Banff, Canada. They lived on moose jerky. She wore the same pair of jeans every day for seven weeks and only had two pairs of undies.

One night, when Penny and Dave were sleeping under the stars, a bear ambled within twenty feet of them. The bear licked the gas tank on their motorcycle and then lumbered into the forest.

I listened with my gaze fixed on the magnificent world beneath my window. The world I was watching couldn't possibly contain lumbering bears or hippies on motorcycles. From my viewpoint, the world below was perfect in every way.

The waning sun was already behind us, low in the west. We rapidly headed into the night. Layers of thick, ethereal clouds formed a puffy, pink-tinted comforter beneath us as our 747 rose above it all.

I watched the night come. Or perhaps I was watching us race into the night. Every so often a bundle of clouds would open, and far below I could spot tiny gatherings of light, evidence of life.

Then I saw it. The moon. Round and unblinking, that mysterious silver orb seemed to race toward us, riding an invisible, celestial current. I watched the moon peek in the window at me. I imagined I could feel its cool, steady light, more fierce and determined than the glow of any night-light. The plane banked slightly to the right. I turned my head to keep an eye on the moon. I watched and watched and then suddenly, in a blink, it was behind us.

I silently recited Ben's favorite nursery rhyme, *Hey, diddle diddle, the cat and the fiddle, the cow jumped over the moon; the little dog laughed to see such sport, and the dish ran away with the spoon.*

I looked out the window again and was certain that the moon now was under us. Turning to Penny with what I'm sure was a look of dumbfounded marvel, I said, "Guess what? We just jumped over the moon!"

Penny laughed. "Like the cow?"

"Yes, like the cow. We jumped over the moon!"

The flight attendant reached to clear my tray, and Penny busted up. "Well, don't look now, but your dish is about to run away with your spoon!"

Our little jokes weren't that funny, but we were so tired they seemed hilarious. We laughed hard, but then I had to excuse myself and stand in line for the rest room. I shifted from right foot to left and looked around at the immense variety of travelers. Did any of them realize we were on the other side of the moon? None of the faces I scanned seemed amazed. I would have to be amazed for all of us. Amazed and delighted and a little bit nervous about being at God's mercy, as Penny called it.

SEVERAL HOURS LATER...

All my private little dreams scattered when the pilot announced our plane couldn't land in Helsinki due to icy high winds. We circled for almost an hour before an announcement came that we would land at a different airport.

"This can't be good," Penny muttered under her breath.

I reached for the guidebook and found a map. "Do you suppose we're going to Stockholm? It looks pretty far away."

Penny studied the map. "Russia looks closer, doesn't it? They wouldn't fly us into Russia, would they?" It had only been a short year or two since the breakup of the former Soviet Union, and Russia wasn't a travel destination for the average American.

Our landing was rough. The plane came down with a thud

on the tires and then bounced up again for three seconds before reconnecting with the runway. Inside our cramped quarters, the passengers responded with a group gasp.

Outside, the sleet came toward us at an angle. As the plane rolled forward, I could barely make out the small terminal's outline.

From all around us came the click of seat belts being unfastened.

The flight attendant spoke over the intercom in three languages. English was the last. By the way people around us were groaning while the message was delivered in the first two languages, we surmised the news wasn't good.

"We ask that you remain in your seats," the voice finally said in English. "We will not be deplaning at this airport. The latest weather reports predict a clearing in the storm. Our pilot has requested clearance to return to Helsinki."

I stared quietly at my hands. The large hook-shaped scar on the back of my right hand looked larger than usual. It had turned a pale, oyster gray color.

I got the scar when I was fifteen and fell against the side of a tractor at my summer job, picking raspberries at Gelson's farm. It took twenty-five minutes to reach the hospital, and I gushed blood all over the front seat of Mrs. Gelson's new powder blue Ford station wagon, even though I was holding the dish towel and pressing hard like she told me to.

Sitting on this icy runway felt a lot like sitting next to Mrs. Gelson in the emergency room. Whatever happened next couldn't possibly be pleasant.

We sat on the runway of the small mystery airport for more than an hour. The flight attendants came by offering coffee.

"Is it okay if we use the rest room?" Penny asked.

"Of course. Please return to your seat, though, as soon as possible. We expect to receive clearance for takeoff soon."

I decided I better go to the rest room with Penny while I had the chance. The gentleman on the aisle stood silently to let us out. All the stalls were occupied. Penny and I stretched without speaking to each other or making eye contact.

"Penny." I touched her shoulder. "When we return to our seats, why don't you take the window seat? I know you said you don't like the window because it gets so cold, but you're welcome to use my coat as a buffer."

Her expression softened. "Are you sure that's okay?"

"Sure, I wouldn't mind. You need a few more inches of breathing space."

"Thanks, Sharon."

The bathroom stall door opened, and I motioned to Penny. "After you."

"Thanks. I owe you one."

That was a crazy thing for Penny to say. She didn't owe me anything. I was the one who was in debt to her for this whole trip.

I tried to lean against the wall to let a young blond woman with a crying baby join me in the crowded space. "He's not very happy, is he?" I asked.

She answered in a language I didn't understand, but when she slid the knuckle of her first finger into his mouth, I asked, "Teething?"

She gave me a weary look and said, *"Ja,"* before shifting the sobbing baby to her other hip. We were communicating in the universal language of all mothers: baby sympathy. My heart went out to her.

I reached over and gently stroked his damp cheek. "It's okay," I said softly. "It's okay." The tyke turned his round moist eyes toward me and stopped crying.

"That's better. You want me to hold you for a little bit so your mommy can have a break?"

I opened my hands, and the mommy gladly let her chunky bundle climb into my arms.

"How old is he?"

The mother shook her head. She didn't understand my question.

"Is he about nine months old?" I shifted the curious fellow to my left hip and held up my fingers as if I were counting.

"Ah! *Ja, nio.*" She held up nine fingers.

"That's what I thought. My first two boys were solid like this, too." I patted his back, and he released a tiny burp.

Penny stepped out of the stall. She looked surprised. "How did you manage to accumulate a baby in the last three minutes?"

"He likes me," I told Penny. "He stopped crying."

The mom spoke again and motioned toward the available toilet stall.

"You go ahead," I said confidently, as if I understood every word she had said. "I'll hold him for you."

Penny stood next to me, staring for a moment. "I'm going back to our seats."

"I'll be——" My response was cut short by a raging wail from baby boy.

Penny gave me a "he's all yours" look and left quickly.

I jostled the little one, touching his cheek and trying to comfort him by saying, "It's okay. Your mommy will be back in a minute."

He tucked his chin and leaned into my shoulder. I patted his back. "There, there. It's okay."

With a stifled sob, his head came straight up, knocking me hard on the chin and causing me to bite my tongue. Then, without warning, the little prince reared back and spewed partially digested airline pretzels and sour milk all down the front of me.

The stall door opened. I held out the baby and motioned with my head so his mom would see the disaster. With profuse apologies in whatever language she spoke, she took her son into the stall and closed the door, and there I stood, aware that a trail of baby barf had found its way under my shirt and was pooling in my bra.

Somehow, when your child throws up on you, it's never as bad as when it's someone else's child.

The second stall door opened, and I rushed in, locked the door, and thought I might be sick from the overpowering smells in the small space. First I tried paper towels to clean up and flushed them before realizing I might clog the whole system. Oh, what a sorry sight I was, trying the dabbing method on my shirt but only making matters worse. I wet more paper towels and then gave up and stripped to the waist.

I had just wrung out my bra when a bright red light flashed. I stared at the light and then looked at my reflection in the mirror.

"What are you doing here?" I asked the woman who was standing topless in front of me in this suffocating, sour bathroom stall, trapped on the runway of some undisclosed airport, which was possibly inside the border of the former Soviet Union, in the middle of an ice storm.

The absurd looking woman in the mirror didn't answer. However, an invisible flight attendant did. In three languages, no less. "Please return to your seat," the voice said over the intercom.

"I would love to return to my seat," I answered politely. "But Houston, we have a problem here."

No one could hear me, of course, but my banter helped me to stay focused. "My shirt is ruined," I went on. "My bra is soaking wet. Can you smell me? I can smell me. If I can smell me, then Penny...well, Penny is..."

I tried to dry my bra by pressing it between two paper towels.

Someone knocked on the bathroom door.

"Yes! I'll be out in just a minute."

"You must return to your seat," the heartless voice said.

"Okay. I'm coming right now."

I still can't believe I did this, but I had no choice. I put on my wet bra and slipped the rancid, damp shirt over my head. Unlocking the door, I made my way back to the center seat with my head down, certain that every eye in that part of the plane was fixed on me. Every nose was probably fixed on me as well.

Poor Penny! The look on her face! She turned away from me, staring out the window as I gave an abbreviated explanation.

I swallowed hard and tried to take tiny breaths. My tongue had swollen from when I bit it right before Junior was sick all over me. I could feel a cold, wet stream zigzagging across my middle and soaking the waistband of my jeans.

The man in the seat directly in front of me stretched to glare at me over the top of his seat.

"I know," I murmured in a tiny voice. "I'm sorry. This isn't exactly pleasant for me either."

Our takeoff was terrifying. The plane seemed to be flapping oversize, weary wings as we rose into the air. We bucked a dozen air pockets, rising and falling like a ship at sea.

Penny grabbed for the bag in her seat pocket and held it

up to her mouth and nose. She didn't get sick, but I'm sure she felt she was about to.

We landed in Helsinki at 7:20 P.M. Without a word, Penny and I walked into the terminal and went directly to the rest room.

"Here." Penny wheeled her suitcase that she carried onto the plane into the first open stall before I could grab some wet paper towels. "Anything you want to wear is yours."

I found a new sympathy for my daughter. *So this is how Kaylee felt when I told her she could wear one of my blouses to the school choir performance.*

Penny's underwear was large on me. Not too large. Just loose and funny feeling. The bra and panties were, however, silky black and a far superior quality to anything I ever owned.

The larger size of her clothes didn't matter because I opted for a baggy pair of sweatpants and a yellow sweater that were easy to pull out of the suitcase.

With my soiled clothes in a wad, I exited the stall to see a line of women waiting. Penny stood near the sinks. "You are going to throw those away, aren't you?"

I hadn't planned on it. I was going to ask if she had a plastic bag. Surely they sold good strong laundry detergent in Finland. I could soak these clothes back to life, if I had the right laundry soap.

Penny moved closer when she saw me stalling. "If I'm right," she said in a low voice, "your bra is at least eight years old, and it's about half an inch from self-disintegrating."

Penny knew all too well the areas in my budget where I'd scrimped over the years to keep four growing children clothed.

"And if I'm guessing correctly, that shirt found its way

into your life in the mideighties. Its shelf life has expired, Sharon. You need to set the poor thing free."

Part of me was glad that Penny felt well enough to be flippant. That was a good sign. But I wasn't too happy about her painfully accurate comments about my wardrobe.

"I'm not trying to be mean," Penny said quickly. "Look, you said you packed plenty of clothes. And I packed way more than I need. We should be fine with what we have until your luggage arrives. If not, we'll go shopping and buy new clothes. Now wouldn't that be tragic?"

I opened the top of the trash bin, and against all my frugal instincts, I threw away a perfectly usable set of clothes.

"Didn't that feel good?" Penny said.

"No. Nothing feels good at the moment." I pushed up the sleeves of the baggy yellow sweater and went to work washing my hands and forearms. My sticky chest and stomach would have to wait. We had an audience in line, and I wanted to get out of there as soon as possible.

"Thanks for letting me borrow your clothes," I said as Penny and I followed the signs to baggage claim. The directions were in three languages, with English the last listed. I noticed how quiet the airport was.

"Of course, you're welcome to borrow anything you want." Penny's voice seemed unusually loud as she turned toward me. "I hate to tell you this, but I can still smell you."

"I know. I need to wash up some more."

"Why didn't you do it back in the rest room?"

"All those women were watching me," I said, lowering my voice.

Penny laughed. "But just think! You could have started your career as an international underwear model."

"Not in your black silkies," I muttered.

"What?" Penny's voice still seemed loud.

I shook my head and mouthed the words, "Never mind." In a whisper I added, "It's so quiet here."

Penny listened a moment. "It is."

We looked around at the people as we walked past the boarding areas. Some were looking back at us. Some were reading. Some were sipping coffee from white ceramic cups at small round tables. No loud announcements were being made. No elevator music filled the air like audio Novocain. We had landed in a somber place.

"This is spooky," Penny muttered. "I'm so used to background noise."

"I think it's serene," I whispered.

My voice must have been too low for her to understand my comment because Penny replied, "I know. It is a scream, isn't it?" She laughed. The sound echoed in the large terminal. Penny covered her mouth with her free hand, and we proceeded to baggage claim.

We didn't realize that we would have to go through customs again. This time they motioned for the two of us to step up to the window together, probably because we seemed to be traveling together.

The officer opened Penny's passport first. He looked up at her and carefully pronounced, "Penny Lane?"

Penny smiled and said flippantly, "Yes, yes, I know. I'm in your eyes and in your ears and under blue suburban skies and all that. Yes, that's my real name."

He didn't blink.

Penny smiled more broadly at the officer. "Aren't you going to start singing to me?"

Silence.

"The Beatles, you know? Penny Lane? Or did the Beatles never make it over here to Helsinki?"

I cringed.

The officer repeated, "Penny Lane?"

"Yes, that's my name. It's my real name. I am Penny Lane."

"Thank you."

"You're welcome."

"Visit to Finland for business or leisure?"

"Leisure."

"Length of stay?"

"About a week and a half."

Without changing his expression, the man stamped her passport and reached for mine.

"Sharon Andrews?"

"Yes."

Unshaken by Penny's vibrant monologue, the officer asked me the same string of questions.

Blessedly, we both made it through customs and arrived at baggage claim. However, my suitcase didn't fare as well.

My luggage didn't make it to Helsinki.

Steal Away

by Linda Hall
ISBN 1-59052-072-6, U.S. Suggested Retail Price: $11.99
290 pages, trade paperback, Fiction/General/Suspense
Reader's Group Discussion Questions Available

May 2003

Dr. Carl Houseman, celebrated minister and speaker, is determined to find out what really happened to his wife, declared dead five years ago after her sailboat washed ashore on a coastal island in Maine. Private investigator Teri Blake-Addison must piece together the life of this woman who felt she didn't know or understand the God that her husband so faithfully served. Did Ellen really die in those cold Atlantic waters? When a murder rocks the island, Teri knows more is at stake than just the puzzling life of an unhappy minister's wife.

❧

"God has put eternity in the human heart" (Ecclesiastes 3:11) By nature we know there is something beyond ourselves, something more to this life than this life. As a writer of fiction, I daily immerse myself in worlds that are beyond my own. My passion, my calling is to help wounded and hurting Christians. Sometimes my imaginary worlds are peopled with dark characters and difficult places, and I must work through these to reveal the Hope on the other side.

It is my prayer that *Steal Away* will take you beyond yourself to where the love of God will show you complete forgiveness.

Linda Hall

SAMPLE CHAPTER

It took her three days to dig the grave. Exhausting work, and made more so by the fact that it could be done only at night. She could not risk Audrey finding out. Better if she didn't know. Better if she lived the rest of her small life not knowing.

"She is gone. She's just gone," is what would be said to the child.

There was no coffin, no satin-lined casket, no memorial service broadcast on national television, no flowers; just a body wound in a new blanket and hidden behind the foundation stones at the back of the house. She had toyed with the idea of taking the body out to sea. There was a wooden dory pulled up on the shore below the cliff. At high tide she could heave it down to the water, place the body inside, and row out as far as she was able.

But that presented its own set of problems. Could she manage to slide the body out of the boat without capsizing it? And what if the body, instead of sinking and burying itself in the layers of bottom mud, washed up on some distant shore, a product of these unpredictable tides and swirling currents? There would be fingerprints, hair and cloth fibers. There were things they could do now, things they could discover. DNA. She had no idea how these things worked, but she couldn't take the risk. There was Audrey to think about. No. Burial in the earth would be a comfort, she thought. No one deserves to die at sea.

The site she chose was a hundred feet up the hillside, protected by trees, and offered a view of the bay. She had walked the length of these, her woods, that bordered the craggy foggy cliffs, and all was sea swept and harsh, save for this one sheltered space. Flowers actually grew here in the summer, and the ground was pliable for digging.

Only once in all of those three nights had she thought she heard a scratching in the underbrush. She had turned, alarmed. But it was merely a deer who looked up at her.

"You will keep this a secret, will you not?" The sound of her own voice startled her. These were the first words she had spoken aloud in many days. Even to Audrey.

The deer turned and bounded away.

At the end of each night's digging, her hands were blistered and raw, and sweat drizzled down her face despite the cold. When the hole was almost waist deep, the woman climbed out and shook off the dirt. But by now it had crusted in the folds of her skin, and she breathed it in through her nostrils with every breath and tasted it with every swallow. She wondered if she would ever forget that peculiar humid aroma of fresh earth.

Down at the cottage it was silent. Audrey would be asleep, her mouth opened, perhaps. She would be jerking a bit in dreams, calling out her unintelligible words. But Audrey was silent tonight, still, and the woman did not know if this boded ill or well.

She bent over the girl's bed, straightened the quilt around her, and with the corner of it swabbed a smear of drool that had settled on her chin.

"Dear sweet one, rest," she whispered. "Mama's here. Mama will always be here. Everything will be all right now." The girl whimpered but did not waken. The woman closed the door soundlessly behind her.

It only remained to carry the body up the hill to the grave. The tide was in, and though she couldn't see the ocean, she heard it, a roar in her ears.

The stiffness had gone out of the corpse and it felt strangely light, as if no longer weighted down by soul and emotion and heart and will. There was a sweet odor about it, which caused the woman's eyes to water, whether from the smell of it or with tears, she couldn't tell. Perhaps both. She cradled the body like you would a child and carried it slowly up the path.

At the place between the trees, she stood for several moments and looked into the hole, considering. She laid the blanket-wrapped body on the ground and climbed into the grave, then she awkwardly pulled the body in after her. She laid it out at the bottom, straightened the limbs, folded the hands across the chest, and covered the face with the blanket. Her movements were instinctive, her thoughts elsewhere. She was eight years old, and she and her father were burying a dead bird that had flown into the picture window. She had cried then, and her father put his hand on her head and said it was okay. All things in God's timing. But she remembered the blue of the feathers, the way the wings folded forward and around the bird. Like a sparrow falling. A woman dead.

She climbed out and began pushing shovelfuls of dirt onto the body, slowly at first, but then more quickly. By the time the gray light of morning was breaking over the sea, it was done.

She knelt for a long time and smoothed the grave over with her hands, smoothing, smoothing her garden. She spread leaves and moss and scrub brush over the top of it, working, raking the clods of earth through her fingers, until only the most astute observer would notice the seam where the earth had been peeled back.

Something should be said, she thought, some memorial, some service. She was openly crying now, sobbing as the magnitude of what she had done came to her. She flung herself across the top of the grave and wept.

My God, my God, why hast Thou forsaken me?

A long while later she rose, wiped her eyes with her dirt-scorched hands, and walked down the path to her house, the sea a pool of molten lead in front of her.

In the kitchen she stripped off her filthy clothing and stood naked on the stone floor, the muddy jeans and flannel shirt in a heap at her feet. She took a rag and drenched it in the cauldron of water on the back of the woodstove. She sopped it over her shoulders, her back, her neck, her face. Her movements were careful, slow, and she wept while she did this. For a long time she wept.

She unclipped, finally, the pins that held up her hair and lined them on the edge of the sink. She ran her fingers through her long, thick, and mostly gray, hair. Clots of dirt and bits of branches fell to the floor.

With the remainder of the water, she washed her hair, getting rid of the last stink of death and dirt. When it was clean she combed it, plaited it, and it hung in one long wet braid behind her back. This one act had sealed it for her. She realized that. She would cry no longer. This would be her life now.

And from this day forward she would mark her times and seasons by the rhythms of the tide and Audrey's rising and lying down. She would spend her days repairing the foundation of her house, poking in rocks and limbs to keep it from crumbling. She would climb to the top of the lighthouse and sit and look at the sea. She and Audrey would gather mussels and dig for clams at the edge of the water when the tide was low. They would fish in the pond behind the house. She would make bread from the flour, butter, and eggs that were delivered weekly from town.

In the spring she would plant flowers on the grave, and each fall the blossoms would die away to be covered by snow. And each spring she would plant them again.

This would be her life now.

"Yes," Teri said to Jack on Saturday morning. "Carl Houseman really wants to meet with me. With us, actually."

"*Dr.* Carl Houseman?" Jack leaned forward in his easy chair and looked over the top of his *Fiddlehead Journal.*

"Well, I don't know if he's the same esteemed man of letters that you're referring to, but yes, someone named Carl Houseman is flying up to meet me—us—today." Teri was repotting houseplants that sat on the kitchen counter like soldiers in a row. She was digging around a small furry-leafed plant with a little trowel.

"From Philadelphia?"

"Yes, from Philadelphia."

"Dr. Carl Houseman from Philadelphia?"

"Yes, Dr. Carl Houseman from Philadelphia."

Jack closed the magazine and folded his hands on top of it. "Teri, do you have any idea who Dr. Carl Houseman from Philadelphia is?"

"Yes, I do, actually. He's a minister with a television program. I was able to get a couple of his books from the church library. I also looked at his website. I've done my research, and I've spent the better part of last week skimming through his books."

"Teri, Carl Houseman is currently one of the most well-known Christian apologists and speakers. His books have sold in the millions."

"I know that. Yes."

"He isn't merely, as you say, a minister with a television program. His church service is broadcast internationally. His opinions are quoted by many. He's been on *Larry King*. He's been to the White House..."

Teri sighed. "I know that. Yes."

"And he wants to hire you?"

"I don't know why you seem so surprised. I'm a highly respected private investigator." The little furry plant was out of its container and would soon happily find a home in another, bigger one. "I need more potting soil," she said. "Remind me to put it on my list for today."

"Don't change the subject. How would he even have heard of you?"

"My reputation precedes me. You want some coffee?"

"Why would he want to hire you?"

"I'm having a cup of coffee. Shall I pour you one, dear?"

"You're changing the subject. If I want coffee I can get it myself. Why would he want to hire you?" Jack was in the kitchen now pouring two cups of coffee, black for himself and a hefty dollop of real cream for Teri.

"I already know why." She said it rather smugly.

"He told you?"

"He didn't have to. I have impeccable research methods. Okay, here it is. Carl Houseman's wife died five years ago, leaving Carl and four sons. The three oldest are married with children. Carl Jr., the eldest, works in the ministry office in Philadelphia, right next to Papa. I'd say he's being primed to take over. His wife's name is Mariana and they have three children; the oldest, a boy, is Carl Houseman III. Second son, Charles, or Charlie as he's known to family and friends, is a missionary in India. He and his wife have two children. Sam, the third son, is a youth minister in a rather large church in Colorado Springs. All of them are doing rather well. Papa and Mama, were she still alive, would be proud of them. It's the fourth son, Brent, the youngest, the baby of the bunch, the prodigal—he left home a year after his mother died." She added spoonfuls of soil to the bottom of a small pot.

"And?"

"Dr. Houseman wants me to find him. And he will be hiring the perfect PI for the job since I know all about prodigals, having been one myself for a whole lot of years. I'm perfect for the job."

"And knowing you, you've already found him."

"His name is Brent Houseman. He's twenty-three years old, lives in Orange, New Jersey. He works at Pizza Hut where his fellow employees describe him as quiet and agreeable, but not opposed to a good party. He's currently living with a twenty-two-year-old waitress named Amanda Mast. He's known to enjoy the occasional beer, but really, his favorite foods are hamburgers and french fries.

"You're amazing."

"I know. One step ahead of your clients. That's my motto. That's why famous people hire me."

She grabbed a piece of paper towel off the roll and wiped her hands. She had repotted two of the furry-leafed little ones with the tiny purple and pink flowers. She had a couple of stripy leafy ones to go, plus a huge tree-like thingy with broad leaves that she would need Jack to help her repot. She collected houseplants like some people collect stamps, but unlike stamp collectors, she knew the names of none of them, nor their particular needs. Sunlight, soil, and water—hey, she'd say, that's what all plants need, right? But, curiously, they flourished in her care. Today in Bangor after the meeting, she'd get a couple of new pots and more potting soil. She started a list.

A week ago, a man with a deep voice and that distinctive Philadelphian accent had called her office, wanting to hire her to look into an extremely confidential and personal matter. "I'll be flying into Bangor next Saturday," he told her. "I'm scheduled to speak at a conference starting Sunday but would love to meet with you and your husband about this."

"My husband?"

"Yes, is he available?"

"I work alone, Dr. Houseman."

"Oh."

"I'm sorry; is there a problem?" The nerve of some men, especially these evangelist types with their antiquated ideas about women. Her husband? Well, if he wanted a man PI, why didn't he phone a man PI in the first place? She was about to say, "I'm sorry, Dr. Houseman; I don't think I'm the person you want for the job," when he said, "I realize that came out wrong, but I have a lot of enemies out there. If someone saw me meeting alone with a private investigator, well, I don't even want to think what they would put together and come up with. Do you understand? If I'm meeting with a couple for dinner, no one would put two and two together and get five."

Oh. "We'd love to meet with you."

Dr. Carl Houseman was also, as Jack pointed out to her the afternoon after the phone call, one of the "good guys." His name had never been linked to any kind of scandal, his reputation never sullied. He had written more than a dozen books that had been described by reviewers as "thoughtful and insightful," and "honest and revealing." As well, he and his late wife had coauthored a couple of bestselling books on marriage and the family. Jack pointed out that his commentary on Jeremiah was one of the standard textbooks in seminaries now. In the past three days Teri had skimmed it. Bible commentaries weren't her regular reading material, but she found this one fascinating, which surprised her.

"Maybe I should go to seminary," she told Jack one evening. "I could be a minister. Would that surprise you?"

"Teri, if there's one thing I've learned in eight months of married bliss with you, it's that there's nothing you could do in this entire world that would surprise me."

In the afternoon they headed into Bangor, a shopping list of plant paraphernalia in Teri's shoulder bag.

Carl Houseman's plane was on time, and Teri immediately recognized him from the picture on his book jacket.

"Dr. Houseman," said Jack, extending his hand, surprised, hesitant. "I'm James Addison. It's a pleasure to meet you."

"And it's a pleasure to meet the two of you." He shook their hands in turn, and Teri thought he had what people in politics pay image consultants good money to get—presence, charisma. They were walking through the airport terminal and talking about flights and time schedules and airline food and how one gets tired of such things after a while.

"I know," Teri said. "I do a fair amount of flying with my work. It's nice to get those airline points, though."

When Dr. Houseman took a side trip into the men's room, Teri grabbed Jack's jacket. "See, it's him. The *real* Dr. Carl Houseman. I told you."

"You're right. I am truly humbled," Jack said. "The famous Christian evangelist and writer wants to hire us."

"Me, Jack. Me."

When Carl returned and his bag was collected, the three of them walked out into the sunshine of a crisp winter day.

"You can sit in the front, Dr. Houseman," Teri said at the car. "Jack'll drive and I'll sit in the back. I don't mind."

"No reason for that. I'll sit in the back. I insist on it. And please call me Carl."

He smiled and she melted. She knew he was more than ten years older than Jack and more than twenty years older than she was. But at fifty-nine, he was fit, handsome, and charming. No wonder he was so successful.

When they were finally in the car, Jack driving and Carl in the back, Jack said, "Do you have a place to stay tonight? Are we taking you anywhere after we eat?"

"I don't have anything booked. No one knows I'm here, actually. The conference doesn't start until tomorrow night. I was hoping you could direct me to a friendly hotel for the night."

"We can do better than that. Would you like to stay with us? We have a huge old house with plenty of rooms. That is, if you don't mind sharing your living space with a couple of old, friendly cats, a dog, and a living room full of houseplants."

Teri sat back in her seat and visualized the place—newspapers all over the floor, dishes in the sink, litter boxes unattended to, bits of dog food all over the linoleum, flowerpots on the kitchen counter, potting soil scattered everywhere...

"If it's no imposition, I'd love that."

...guest room bed needing the sheets changed, carpets needing vacuuming, nothing in the fridge to eat...

"It's no imposition at all. We insist."

"Yes, we insist," Teri added.

The Lights of Tenth Street

by Shaunti Feldhahn

ISBN 1-59052-080-7, U.S. Suggested Retail Price: $14.99
500 pages, trade paperback, Fiction/General/Contemporary
Reader's Group Discussion Questions Available

May 2003

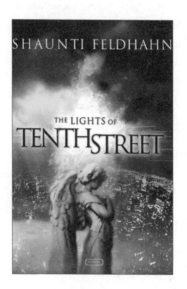

Follow the intersecting lives of a beautiful young woman captured by the sex industry, a suburban Christian couple trapped by complacency, and the heavenly forces fighting to set them both free.

🌿

Before I began this book, I had never given much thought to the issues raised in this book about the sex industry—from the difficult struggles that so many devoted Christian men have with their thought lives, to the young women caught in the grip of the "exotic dancer" clubs. I guess I just believed—as many of us do—that it was not touching me or my community personally. What I didn't realize was that this industry impacts all of us in both subtle and pervasive ways, whether we are aware of it or not.

Further, although I knew that Jesus befriended prostitutes and others ostracized by society, I could never (to my shame) imagine myself doing the same. Now, after a year of research and writing, I count a number of former strippers as dear friends. And I realize that even in the depths of their entrapment in that life, that they were normal people caught in an abnormal situation. That is not to excuse sin, but when we recognize that everyone has a story, it is much easier to look on them and love them as a person, rather than focusing solely on their behavior.

The genesis of *The Lights of Tenth Street* arose from hearing the Christian testimony of a former stripper and prostitute. She had grown up in a small, depressed town, was sexually assaulted as a teenager, and was lured into the strip club life thinking it would be a glamorous way to make lots of money. Instead, it was depraved and awful, a dead-end trap. After she had spent years in that life, a Christian woman in her neighborhood knocked on her door, inviting her to her church's Christmas banquet. And when she took her up on it, to her immense surprise, she found nothing but love and acceptance in their church, even though she didn't know how to dress or act. That former stripper now has a wonderful ministry to other strippers and prostitutes.

When I heard that story, I somehow knew that the Lord was nudging me to write a book that would feature just such a girl, to show the incredible transforming power of unconditional, nonjudgmental love. But that wasn't all. As the months passed, I realized that the flip side of this sort of story—the consumer's side—leaves in its wake many devastated men (and, increasingly, even women) who have been ensnared by pornography. So there had to be two character plotlines—one to follow the young stripper, the other to follow the Christian couple who will eventually reach out to her...but to do so, the husband has to confront his own secret addiction.

When I started the book, these issues weren't even on my radar screen. But they just kept getting bigger and bigger. I was truly shocked to realize the depth of this problem in our culture, including among devoted Christian men.

I think it is safe to say, however, that what shocked me as a woman would be no surprise to any man on the planet. And I bet that many of my female readers are in the same boat. I knew, of course, that men and women are different. But as I tried to get inside my male character's head, my eyes were dramatically opened to just *how* different!

It has become one of my main prayers that the Lord will use this book to open the eyes of women, that we might understand the cultural and personal battle all around us...including one that almost certainly affects the men and boys that we love. And it is also my prayer that the Lord will use this book to open *all* eyes to the need to reach out and love those who are lost and hurting—just as Jesus would.

Shaunti Feldhahn

Sample Chapter

"You be good, pumpkin."

Ronnie leaned into the broad chest as the owner of the deep voice knelt for a hug by the driveway. She squeezed her arms tight around his waist, breathing in the scent of sawdust and engine oil. She stood quiet in his embrace until she felt him kiss the top of her head. Her fingers gripped tighter.

"Do you have to go? Can't I go with you just this once?"

"Nope." The calloused hands gently pried her fingers loose. "I told your mom I'd have you back by five o'clock. It's already past that. I hope you had fun with the other kids at that church, at least."

"I did!" The little face beamed. "That teacher lady this morning told us a story about how this man got beat up by some bad guys, and how another good man helped him. She said I was kind, like the good man!"

She prattled on about her morning. He finally stood up, silencing her. Then he took one of her hands in each of his and gave her a small smile. He chucked her under the chin, his voice quiet.

"Go on in now, Raggle-bear. I love you."

Out of the corner of her eye, Ronnie saw movement at the front curtains. She took a step backward.

"I love you too, Daddy."

He climbed into the familiar sedan, and she waved good-bye as the only father she'd ever known backed down the driveway.

Bye, Daddy…

She heard the screen door squeak open behind her, heard

the familiar female voice.

"Come on in, sweetheart."

She turned and shouldered her small bag, then clambered up the uneven porch steps. She accepted another hug, a kiss on the cheek.

"Oh, I *missed* you. Go on now, put your stuff away. Then set the plates for dinner."

Ronnie started to walk around the corner just as another figure appeared in the kitchen doorway.

"Hello, Veronica."

She looked up at the tall man in the doorway, squinting against the ceiling light. "Hi Seth."

His expression darkened. He glanced at her mom, still standing by the front door, and then back at her. His voice was calm. "I have told you repeatedly to call me Dad."

Ronnie looked back down. "I have to go put my stuff away."

Seth stared at her a moment longer, then waved a hand. Ronnie hastened down the hallway toward her room. She put away her pajamas, a few toys, and the white teddy bear that went with her everywhere, and then headed back toward the kitchen.

The swinging door was slightly ajar, and Ronnie could hear voices lowered in intense conversation. She padded softly down the hallway.

"But, Seth, she—"

"No. That's it. He's dangerous to this family, and I won't stand for it."

"But it'll *kill* her not to—"

"So you want to risk it, is that what you're saying?" Seth's voice rose just slightly. "I saw the bruises he left on you. You want that to happen to Veronica?"

Ronnie stopped a few feet from the kitchen door, eyes wide, straining to listen.

"He wouldn't do that to Ronnie."

"And that's another thing. You need to get over this juvenile nickname. Her name is Veronica. She's almost eight, for crying out loud. The sooner we stop mollycoddling her, the quicker she'll grow up and accept her new life."

"But to cut off all visitation—"

"Tomorrow morning," the voice lowered again, "you call the court. It shouldn't take long to convince the judge, once you show your police pictures. Especially since he's not even her biological father."

There was a long silence, and Ronnie stood still, trembling, afraid to move. *Daddy!*

"I can't—I can't do that. She needs her father."

"If you won't, I will. *I'm* her father now, and it'll be better for her if she's not confused by two loyalties. Discussion over."

Seth pushed through the swinging doors, heading toward the living room. He saw Ronnie at the entrance to the hallway, and stopped.

He gave her a long look, then walked toward her. He crouched down and put a hand on her arm.

"Veronica, were you eavesdropping on us? Did you hear that?…Veronica?"

Ronnie could only stare at him. Her eyes turned toward the kitchen doorway where her mother had appeared, pain and defeat etched into her expression. Ronnie's lips began to tremble.

Her arm began to throb, and she realized that Seth had tightened his grip. He was gazing at her with a strange look, his eyes wandering over her face.

"Veronica, don't ignore me."

A dim voice from the kitchen. "Seth, don't."

"Veronica, I asked you a question. If you don't obey, there are consequences."

Her tongue was stuck. Even when he stood up and pulled off his belt, she was frozen. Even when he turned her against the wall and her tears dripped to the carpet. Her mind was numb.

Daddy...

A shining figure bowed his head, his voice soft with grief. "The heavenly Father weeps for His child."

Another great being, his high-ranking garments glinting like the sun, stepped forward. "And another spirit is wounded. Loriel, she is now your charge. You have been chosen to lead this campaign."

"Yes, General." The first angel nodded his acceptance, but his eyes remained fixed on the scene before him. Then he sighed, repeating the man's words in a low voice. *"If you don't obey, there are consequences."* He shook his head. "If the Father's children don't obey *His* heart, there are indeed consequences. But the consequences fall not just upon themselves. The sins of the earthly fathers truly are passed down for generations."

"But God has promised that the righteous will inherit His blessing down to the thousandth generation! His mercy triumphs over judgment."

The two angels watched the little girl retreat to her bedroom and crawl under the covers.

Loriel's eyes darkened as he felt again the pain of the One he was created to serve, the Father's grief over a child's suffering.

"Loriel, this cycle must be broken. The consequences of

this campaign are great, greater perhaps than we have seen since the battles for the establishment of this one nation under God. The enemy's plan is massive, but he is prideful, assured of his success in twisting the hearts and minds of men to destruction. He is expecting opposition, but he is not prepared for the war to be fought apart from his usual front. And on that front lies our hope."

Loriel looked back to the small girl sniffling under the covers. "If only they will listen."

The General smiled and laid a strong hand on his arm. "That, too, is your charge." He stepped back and gave the traditional salute. "It is time, Commander. You must be strengthened for this journey. Clothe yourself in the armor of God!"

Loriel lifted his head and opened his arms wide. A melody of praise poured forth from his lips, catching him up before the Throne. He lost himself in the beauty and the power of worship before his Maker, captivated by the glory of the Ageless One. He could feel himself growing strong with the power of the Spirit, his wings unfurling with sparks like lightning.

How long he reveled in worship he did not know, but the time came—as it always did—when he felt the Lord's release. He was created for the fight, but still he longed to stay before the Throne, longed for the day when all creation would bow before the humble King.

And his purpose was to hasten that day. Loriel bent his knee and heard his call.

As I set aside My glory and dwelt in the land of the shadow, so must My servants also go. The darkened lands are thirsting for My living water. I am calling to My bride, My church! Carry My message! And minister...minister to My precious lambs.

Loriel closed his eyes at his Master's longing for those He

had died to save. A heavenly resolve began to burn in his breast, and he lifted his head, his eyes fierce with determination. He was created to serve and protect these who were so precious to his King!

He launched himself upward, a great cry on his lips as a shining host rallied to his call. They wore no weapons, for the Prince of Peace was their standard. This campaign was not yet a battle against the enemy. This campaign was to awaken a sleeping bride.

HIGH SCHOOL. TEN YEARS LATER...

Ronnie ran her last lap with the other girls, grateful that the physical effort spared her from thinking. A girl in front glanced toward the stands, and despite herself, Ronnie's head jerked sideways. The two men in the stands were still intent in conversation with their coach.

All three pairs of eyes were fastened on her.

Ronnie looked forward and tried to keep an even pace. She could hear her heart thudding, feel her ponytail swinging at her back. *Please...please...*

The pack reached the stopping point and tailed off, each girl slowing, walking, hands on hips, taking subtle gasps of air and trying to look as if they ran that pace every day before breakfast.

Ronnie leaned forward and stretched her back and legs, then kept walking, moving easily in the warm-ups each cheerleader wore on cool days. It would be December soon. The end of the season; no more Friday-night games.

She glanced toward the stands again, her skin prickling in the cold. She tried not to fidget. She'd made it this far; maybe fate would make a way.

There was a sudden murmuring among the girls. The coach was climbing slowly down from the stands, her face shadowed. Ronnie hardly listened to his words. "Each of your routines was great, but at this time..."

The two men gathered their things and headed toward the parking lot, taking her college dreams with them.

The other cheerleaders shared disappointed chatter as they collected their books and clothes from the locker room. One or two patted Ronnie on the arm as they passed. "If anyone would've made it, it would've been you..."

Ronnie exchanged pleasantries, unable to remember a moment later what she had said. She slung her backpack over her shoulder as her friends climbed into the cars waiting in the parking lot; their parents', their boyfriends', their own.

She started on the long walk home, thinking of Tiffany's e-mail that morning. Maybe a blond ponytail and blue eyes could do what fate couldn't.

A brassy car horn broke Ronnie out of her reverie as she waited to cross the street.

"Hey, Ronnie! Need a ride?" An elderly grocer she'd known since childhood was leaning out his pickup truck's window.

"No thanks, Mr. Dugan." She smiled at the old man. "I'm almost home."

"Come on, Ronnie. I know you better than that. You still got two, three miles yet." He leaned over and swung the creaky door wide.

Ronnie hesitated, then sighed and clambered up into the truck. "I am pretty tired. And I do have to work tonight. Thanks."

"I'm heading past your place anyway. As long as you don't

mind if I take five minutes to drop off some equipment on the way."

"No problem." Ronnie sank back into the cracked vinyl seat with a sigh of gratitude.

They rode in silence as they approached the center of town. There wasn't much traffic. The McDonald's and the liquor store were doing a brisk evening business, but few cars lined the strip of other storefronts. Even the parking lot of the local supermart— once, the town's main attraction—was sparsely populated. A sheet of plywood had recently gone up over the entrance to the dance studio where she had spent so much of her time.

"So you just come from cheerleading practice?" Mr. Dugan asked.

"No...not exactly."

"You look like you did."

"Yeah." Ronnie looked out the window.

"I've known you since you were born, child. What's wrong?"

Tears crept into the corner of her eyes, and she kept her head turned so the old man couldn't see her face.

"I just..." She took a deep breath and tried again. "I just lost my last chance at a college scholarship." She saw Mr. Dugan look sideways in silence, giving her time to form the words. "One of the big state schools has this famous cheer-leading team, and they hand out scholarships every year. They just had tryouts. None of us made it."

"Ronnie, I'm sorry. I didn't realize you wanted to go to college."

"Well, I do." Tears threatened to erupt again. "I have to. I *have to*. Look at this place, Mr. Dugan!" She jabbed her finger toward the windshield. "Half the storefronts are boarded up.

And all my classmates want to do is hang out in the McDonald's parking lot and smoke weed."

She caught herself and glanced sideways. "Oh—I probably shouldn't say that in front of you."

He gave her a sad smile. "It's not like it surprises me, Ronnie."

"And then they'll have babies too early, or get stuck in some minimum-wage job at the factory for the rest of their lives." She closed her eyes. "I want *more* than that! I want to get out and do something important, something that helps people."

"Like what?"

Ronnie didn't answer for a moment, then she continued in a quiet voice. "About three years ago, I hurt my back really bad in that car accident."

"I remember. You had that cast thing on for a while."

"Yeah. Well, it only got worse, even though I saw a couple of doctors about it. Finally, someone referred me to this physical therapist. She worked with me for a whole year, until I was back to normal. And she didn't even charge me the whole fee, only what the insurance would cover from the jerk that hit me. That's the kind of thing I want to do. That therapist knew so much cool stuff, and she could help people with it! I don't want to work at the pizza place for the rest of my life. I don't want to end up stuck here like—"

She caught herself before the words slipped out. *Like my mother...*

Mr. Dugan glanced at her and then looked back at the road. The wheels of the truck bumped over the entrance to a small parking lot, and he steered the truck to a gentle stop.

"I'll be back in a jiffy."

Ronnie watched in the rearview mirror as the elderly

man began hauling a heavy industrial cooler out of the back of the truck. She jumped out and ran around to the back.

"That's so heavy! Can I help—"

Mr. Dugan braced the chest against the tailgate and lowered it to the ground. He grinned at her as he slid a dolly under its base, secured it with a few straps, and wheeled it away, whistling to himself.

She watched him go, heading toward "Big Al's Fix-It Shop." The other storefronts had worn signs proclaiming "Shepherd Christian Books—*All Your Christian Needs for Less*," "Oasis Tanning Salon," and "Guns Galore—*Guns Guns Guns!*"

She rolled her eyes and climbed back into the pickup. Maybe she should think about changing jobs. Tiffany had hated working at the tanning salon, but sure had loved looking sun-bronzed in the dead of winter.

Ronnie made a face. Just another dead-end job. Why was it that she was the only one of her friends who wanted to look beyond the next paycheck, the next boyfriend? Last year when she'd had her final back checkup, she had sat in her doctor's private office and stared, transfixed, at the diplomas on the wall, the books on the shelves behind his desk. She listened, envious, as he rattled off the dosage and instructions for patients' medicine from memory. Now *he* was making a difference and helping people and making great money at the same time. Just like her physical therapist. They weren't trapped: They could do anything they wanted to do.

Why on *earth* were they doing it in this town?

The driver's door creaked open and Mr. Dugan settled in behind the wheel. "Okay. We're out of here."

He started the engine and feathered the clutch just so. As the old pickup got underway, he continued their conversation as if they had never stopped.

"You know, my daughter-in-law—Angela Dugan—is a guidance counselor at your school."

"I've seen her a couple times."

"Why don't you go talk to her tomorrow? Maybe she'll have some ideas for you. I know she'll appreciate your desire to go to college. She went to college, you know. The only one of us to go."

"Really? Where?"

"Georgia State."

Ronnie's eyes widened. "Georgia State! That's where—I mean, I had been thinking about Georgia State, too. But if I don't have a scholarship, I'll have to put myself through school."

"Atlanta isn't cheap, you know."

Ronnie looked down at her hands. "Yeah, I know."

A few minutes later, the pickup pulled up a narrow side road and stopped. Ronnie gave Mr. Dugan a quick hug and hopped out by a row of mailboxes down the road from her house, glad that excuse had come to mind.

She waved as the truck drove away, collected a short stack of mail, and headed down the road for home.

"Well, I don't *care* what you think!" Ronnie's eyes snapped across the kitchen. "I can finish high school by GED and start at Georgia State in the fall if I work enough."

Her mother shook her head, grinding a cigarette into an ashtray on the counter. "You can get a job here and start college next year if you're still so wild about it. It's not like you've got anything special to offer an employer. So there's no need to go so far for work."

Ronnie made an exasperated noise. "Give me a break. You

know how hard it is to find a good job these days! And I'm a hard worker, but there's certainly no work in this town that would pay enough for me to *live* on, much less save for college."

"You can live here."

"No, I can't. And you know that." She tried to hold her mother's gaze, but the tired eyes flickered down and away. The kitchen was silent a moment.

Her mother reached for the half-crinkled pack lying on the counter beside her, and turned slightly to light another smoke.

Ronnie opened the refrigerator door, looking for something to eat. "At least the beer is still here from this morning," she muttered. "That's something."

"Seth bought a new six-pack before you got home."

Ronnie pulled a lone apple from the crisper drawer, then set about searching the cupboards for the box of macaroni and cheese she knew was there somewhere. She made and ate her dinner silently, sitting at the kitchen table and staring out at the lawn. Her mother retreated into the living room to watch television, leaving Ronnie alone.

Could she do it? Did she have the guts? Would her friends miss her? She looked down at her plate, her stomach sinking. Did she have any choice?

The sound of a souped-up engine broke her spell, and she moved quickly over to the sink, rinsing her plate and putting it in the dishwasher. She heard the screen door slam shut and Seth's heavy steps into the kitchen.

"I thought I told you to clean the kitchen this morning."

She kept her back to him, rinsing a few of the dishes stacked in the sink. "You did. But I had school, and then the cheerleading tryouts. I just got back."

He walked over and gripped her arm, swinging her

unsteadily around. "Don't you get lippy with me, young lady."

She yanked her arm out of his grasp and glared at him, her breath catching in her chest. "You've been drinking, Seth. Why don't you just go sleep it off?"

"Why you—" He slapped her across the cheek. "Why don't you just sleep *that* off?"

Ronnie stepped back, her face stinging, then pushed past him and headed down the hall. Her mother never looked up from the television.

She swept into her room, closed the door and locked it, then turned and kicked it with her foot, hard. She flopped down beside the bed and pressed a hand to her cheek, trying not to cry. Just another day in the Hanover family. If you could call this a family.

She pictured her coach addressing the rejected cheerleaders, and a wave of despair swept over her. Was she *ever* going to be anybody? Maybe she was just fooling herself. Maybe she should just accept the fact that there was nothing special about her.

She scooted over to her nightstand, opened the bottom drawer, and lifted out a weathered shoebox. She leaned back against the bed, and opened the lid. A white teddy bear, well-loved and worn in patches, stared up at her.

Ronnie smiled and pulled him out. Teddy had a lot of secrets on him, a lot of comforted tears. She set him aside and felt in the box for the folded paper she knew was there.

It was yellowed with age, soft and brown and worn from many creases, many foldings and unfoldings. Ronnie carefully spread the page on her lap, pondering the familiar words, surrounded by little drawings and stickers; perfect for a second-grade child.

Ronnie, I'm very glad you and your father joined us at church today! Although you just came to my Sunday school class for the first time, I can tell there is something special about you. You have a kind heart. I watched you help and comfort that little boy when he cut himself, and it is clear that you have a gift. A gift of healing, of helping people. Just like in the story of the Good Samaritan, you care about other people and it shows.

I don't know how long you and your dad will be with our church. I'd love to have you every week. But just in case, I wanted you to know that you are a special girl, and Jesus loves you very much. Don't ever let anyone take that away from you.

A chime from the computer made Ronnie turn, and she carefully refolded the page and stowed it in its hiding place. She checked her e-mail and smiled. Now here was another person who had believed in her...even if some of her crazy plots were a little unorthodox. Including the one she was pushing at the moment. Ronnie clicked on Tiffany's e-mail.

Where are you girl? I've been trying to instant-message you all afternoon!

Listen, you need to stop thinking so much and just do it. Now that your man is history, you've got no reason to stay. I'll be back in town on Friday to close my bank account and all that, so you can come back to Atlanta with me. Otherwise, you'll just have to find a ride or pay for the train, and I know you don't have the money.

One look at the car I'm driving, you'll wonder why you waited so long. I told Marco and the others that you're finally considering it, and we can set up an interview as soon as you arrive. I know they'll love you. I'm only worried that once they check you out, I'm history! Just kidding. Sort of.

Anyway, you know you need to get out of there, so make like Nike. I'll see you Friday.

Ronnie laughed when she reached the end of her friend's message. Well, why not.

She stood up from the computer and started rummaging in her closet for a duffel bag. Tiffany was right. She thought too much, worried too much, planned too much. There was nothing for her here. Not one of her girlfriends really knew her. And her boyfriend was pretending she wasn't even there. She finished loading up her duffel bag, stowed it out of sight, and got ready for another night at her busy, dead-end job.

There was no more reason to stay, and—she shuddered slightly at the thought of Seth's probing eyes—every reason to go.

The Breaking Point

by Karen Ball
ISBN 1-59052-033-5, U.S. Suggested Retail Price: $12.99
400 pages, trade paperback, Fiction/General/Contemporary
Reader's Group Discussion Questions Available

May 2003

Gabe and Renee Roman are on the edge—relation-ally and spiritually. Both are Christians. But after years of struggling in their marriage, their greatest test comes in the most unexpected of forms: a blizzard in the Oregon mountains. Their truck hurtles over the side of a mountain, and each encounters the realities of suffering, sacrifice, and service in Christ's name. It isn't until they surrender their last defenses that their surface understandings are torn away and all that's left is truth: Only through obedience to God's call can they find true joy.

My whole life, all I ever wanted was a marriage like my parents'—full of love and laughter, with God as the foundation and friendship, the cement. Instead, my marriage was full of anger and frustration, with resentment the foundation and "my rights" the barrier keeping us apart.

After many years of struggle, God finally reached Don and me with His call to obedience. As we surrendered our "rights" to Him and strove to serve each other—sometimes through gritted teeth—we discovered the love and marriage we always wanted! Now, after nearly twenty-four years of marriage, Don is my anchor, my confidante, my love.

Many—including Francine Rivers, Angela Hunt, and Robin Jones Gunn—encouraged me to write about God's work in our marriage. But it wasn't until I heard about more and more marriages falling apart that God nudged me. It was time. After much prayer with Don, *The Breaking Point* emerged. This story is based on real experiences—ours and many others whose lives have been a proving ground for God's faithfulness.

We hope it will speak to those who face struggles in their lives and relationships, who are discouraged because life hasn't turned out as they'd dreamed or planned. And we hope it will touch anyone who longs to draw closer to God, to understand His heart. May it encourage and uplift and help others discover what Don and I did: Marriage isn't about being happy as much as about being obedient to the One who calls us together.

Above all, the message of *The Breaking Point* is this: God is sufficient. No matter what. If we will walk in obedience, God will give us all we ever longed for. And more.

Karen Ball

SAMPLE CHAPTER

DECEMBER 19, 2003
10 A.M.

We're out of control.

Renee Roman leaned her forehead against the cold glass of the truck window, her teeth clenched, a barrier against the tears scalding the backs of her eyes. She would not cry. She'd cried enough for a lifetime.

Two lifetimes.

She focused on the winter storm screaming just outside her window. A dense blanket of wind-whipped snow surrounded the pickup as they crept along. Visibility was nil, and gusts of wind buffeted the truck, slamming against it with seemingly determined efforts to knock them sideways.

A whiteout. How fitting. Now they could be as blind to the road as they were to each other...

Hurt tugged at her, and she pressed her lips tight against it. Blind or not, nothing was going to stop them, no sirree. Let the storm rage; their truck would still keep its steady, slow progress. Wind and snow were no match for Gabe. Nothing stopped him when he was determined—no human, no natural disaster, no act of God...

Renee's fingers curled around her seat belt. Here they were, on a treacherous road, at the mercy of the weather, and all Gabe could do was keep moving forward. No stopping to reconsider, no looking for shelter, and certainly no asking for help. Just push your way through and make everything and everyone bend to *your* will.

If she weren't so terrified, the situation would be hilarious.

A small whine drew her attention to the backseat, and she turned to place a comforting hand on Bo's furry head. Funny—Siberian huskies looked so imposing, so fierce, but under that wolflike appearance, they were serious wimps. "It's okay, boy." She uttered the soothing words, doing her best to keep her own anxiety from tainting her tone. "You're fine. We'll be home soon."

If only she believed that. A glance told Renee that Gabe was tense, too, but she knew his tight jaw had little to do with the weather. She buried her fingers in Bo's thick coat. If only she could bury her feelings as completely.

I hate him.

The words, which had nudged her heart and mind since that morning despite her stubborn refusal to grant them entrance, finally took wing.

She knew it was because of the anger. And the terror. She hated driving in the snow. Usually avoided it at all costs—which put driving in a blinding blizzard in the Oregon mountains in the "Things I Utterly Detest" category—but Gabe had been adamant. And nothing she said—no pleas to wait a day, no appeals to reason or compassion—had made a difference.

Oh, he had a list of reasons: They couldn't afford another night in the hotel; he didn't have any more vacation days and couldn't afford a day off without pay; all they had to do was leave early enough to beat the worst of the storm…

But Renee knew the real reason they were on the road in the worst storm of the year. Her husband couldn't wait to get home, to get this miserable trip over with.

To get away from her.

Tears pricked at her eyelids, and she blinked them away.

He wanted to get away from her? Well, that was just fine. She was more than ready to escape his rigid, cold presence. The plummeting temperatures outside the truck cab were a virtual heat wave compared to the frigid atmosphere inside. Neither of them had spoken a word for the past half hour.

Her lips trembled. Why say anything now? They'd said enough—more than enough—that morning.

She gave Bo a final pat and turned to stare out the windshield again, then grabbed the door handle when another blast of wind rocked the cab. She started when Gabe's hand closed over hers. Swallowing a sudden jumble of emotions, she glanced at him. He kept his eyes fixed on the windshield as he spoke.

"Breathe, Renee. I need you to breathe."

She hadn't realized she'd been holding her breath. Amazing. Even in the face of a storm—both physical and emotional—Gabe was still so tuned in to her...

She forced out her pent-up air, then drew in a slow, deep breath.

Gabe squeezed her hand with gentle pressure. "We'll be okay." His gaze brushed hers, then returned to the road.

Fear, frustration, regret, sorrow...one sensation chased another, rippling through her until they were a bitter taste in her mouth.

How did we get here? How do we keep ending up in this place?

She clenched her eyes as the desperate thought scraped at too-raw nerves. They'd been through so much...worked so hard...and she thought they were doing better. Had even dared to believe they'd make it. This whole trip to the mountains to rent a cabin was supposed to be a kind of celebration for them, a rejoicing in all they'd overcome—in all that ten years of counseling had helped them resolve.

So why had it come to this again? To this place of hurt and frustration? This place of cold distance?

Misunderstanding and miscommunication had opened the door to hurt feelings. Angry words followed, bringing resentments Renee thought were long ago resolved. Even now, thinking back on the last few days, Renee couldn't believe it took mere moments for their hard work—and her hope— to shatter. Now the tiny, jagged fragments worked their way deep into her heart; cutting, piercing, wounding her in ways she thought she'd never have to feel again.

Renee wanted to be angry. To yell and scream and throw things. But she had to acknowledge she felt only one thing: grief. Deep, wrenching grief. She stared out the window, blinking against the glaring white—and against scalding tears.

The question came again; this time she gave it voice. "How did we get here, Gabe?"

He didn't answer right away, but his jaw muscles flinched. For once, she waited. Not because she didn't have anything to say, but because she couldn't speak past the tightness in her throat.

"It's the road home."

Leave it to Gabe to give her a literal answer to a question that was anything *but* that. *Please, Gabe, please...listen with your heart instead of your logic.* "That's not what I meant—" the words came out soft and weary—"and you know it."

Exasperation escaped him in a snort. "Right. Whatever you say, Renee."

"Gabe—"

His glare cut her short. "Forget it. Whatever you meant, I don't know the answer, okay? I never do." He turned back to stare at the road. "Not the one you want, anyway."

Bo's nose pressed against her shoulder, halting the angry words she wanted to spew. She reached back and felt his trembling, then released her irritation in a huff. Amazing how connected to them this dog was. He was so tuned in to any tension between her and Gabe. All it took was a raised voice, a hardened tone, and he was there; pacing, looking from one to the other with that wide-eyed anxiety. He'd become a kind of emotional barometer, an alarm to warn them when things were getting out of hand.

Like now.

"You're fine, Bo. Settle down."

At the harsh command, Renee felt her teeth grind and forced her jaw to relax. Did Gabe really believe using that tone would comfort the poor animal? She wanted to tell him how idiotic such a notion was, but as she opened her mouth, Bo commando-crawled between the seats until his upper body rested on the console and leaned into her.

"You'd probably better snap him into his safety harness, Renee."

As much as she didn't want to do so, Gabe was right. The harness attached to the seat belt in the backseat, and it would keep Bo from being thrown if anything should happen.

Nothing's going to happen, her mind scolded her as she unbuckled her own belt and secured Bo. If only she could believe it.

Renee turned back to her seat and refastened her belt, trying to ignore the whining now coming from the backseat. Few sounds were more pitiful than a Siberian's soulful whine, and it did what Renee's conscience couldn't: It kept her quiet.

The silence in the cab grew until Renee thought she would scream. Anything to drown out the thoughts that raged at her, shredding her already wounded heart.

He doesn't care…he can't even stand to look at you, let alone talk to you…he's so wrapped up in his anger that there's no room left for you. For anyone. It's just him and that stupid, hateful temper…

Renee closed her eyes against despair. *Father God, what do I have to do? I've made changes…Gabe's made changes…we've tried.We really have. But what good has it done?We always seem to end up in the same terrible place…* Her throat constricted. *What else can we do?*

One word whispered through her in response: *Die…*

Renee's eyes flew open at that. Die? She glanced out the window, painfully aware that was a too-real possibility right now, given the storm and the winding mountain roads they were on. One wrong turn, one jerk of the wheel at the wrong moment, and they'd be history…a pile of twisted metal at the bottom of a frozen mountain.

She shook the image away. That wasn't the answer. It couldn't be. So what—?

A sudden cry from Gabe was her only warning. That and the sickening sensation of traction suddenly lost…of wheels no longer gripping the road…of control being ripped away…

"Renee! Hold on!"

She scarcely had time to grip the door handle before they were in a spin. She'd always heard that, in moments of crisis, everything seemed to go into slow motion, but she knew now that was wrong. Things sped up. In the space of a heartbeat, their spiraling vehicle slammed into the snowdrift at the side of the road—the only barrier between them and a sheer drop-off. Ice and frozen snow shattered with a force that reverberated in Renee's very bones. She knew, with an odd sense of calm, the moment they broke through…the moment they were airborne…the moment they began to slide down the mountainside...

She didn't have time to be afraid. To think. All she could do was turn to Gabe. What she saw reflected in those blue eyes—eyes that had captivated her the first time he'd looked at her—made everything slow...stop...

Sorrow stared out at her—regret for all they'd said, all they'd never have the chance to say—and a longing so intense she thought it would break her heart.

Renee reached for him, then cried out—when a thunderous jolt slammed her back against the pickup door. For a moment, there was nothing but searing pain.

Then there was nothing.

11:15 A.M.

Dark.

Cold.

Pain.

Each sensation whispered over Renee, drawing her into awareness, away from the stillness.

"No..."

Did she speak the word or just think it? Either way, it seemed to echo through her, a sound as brittle and frightened as any she'd ever known.

Her eyelids dragged open, and she blinked against the brightness, battling the fog that seemed to fill her mind as well as her vision. But what she saw didn't make any sense.

White. Everything was bathed in white. There was a suffocating blanket of it outside the truck, where snow blew and swirled. And inside the truck...the white was there, too. On the windshield...in the air...

As Renee's dazed eyes focused, she saw why. Snow was piled on the dashboard, on her lap, and every time she exhaled, a white puff filled the air. She drew a deep breath, but as the frigid air flowed into her lungs, she was seized by a fit of coughing that racked her body.

As she struggled to breathe, she realized how cold she was. So cold she couldn't stop shivering. "G...Gabe?"

A flash of red and white came into view, and she pulled back just as Bo vaulted the seat backs and landed half in her lap, half on the floor. His frantic tongue bathed her face, and Renee grabbed at his front paws as they raked her shoulders.

"Bo, *no!* Down!"

True to his training, the husky sat with a thump on the floorboard at Renee's feet. But he leaned into her, his two-colored stare fixed on her like a child seeking comfort after waking from a nightmare. Renee dug her cold hands into his fur, scratching his neck, trying to comfort him even as she struggled to understand what had happened.

Her gaze roamed the cab of the truck...and realization seeped in. They'd gone over the edge of the road. The momentum of their spin had slammed them right through the wall of snow and ice at the road's edge. They must have gone down the mountainside...

As the reality of their situation hit her, she turned with a jerk. Sweet relief made her weak when she saw Gabe. Though he was unconscious, puffs of white hanging in the air near his mouth bore blessed testimony to the fact that he was breathing.

"Gabe?" She reached for him, then halted when pain stabbed through her, sucking the air from her lungs, making everything go faint. She drew in shallow gulps of oxygen, fighting to stay conscious.

She reached again, frustrated with her sluggish motions, as though trapped in some slow-motion segment of a movie. She crept her fingers along until they found Gabe's wrist and searched, pressed...

Yes! A pulse. When she felt it pound, strong and steady, she let herself cry.

Thank You, God...thank You...

She leaned her head back against her seat, staring up at the ceiling of the truck cab, then looked down at Bo, who watched her every move. "It's not crushed or caved in at all." She felt the ceiling. "We must not have rolled. Well, that's a blessing anyway." She shifted her gaze and grimaced. The front of the truck was another story. It looked as if it had been put in some gigantic trash compactor. Clearly it had taken the brunt of their landing.

They must have slid down the side of the mountain, taking out some of the small trees in their path. The front of the truck was accordioned back to the cab—but not into it, thank heaven, or she and Gabe might well have been crushed. Their legs surely would have been.

She glanced at Bo again and saw that his safety harness had been torn, though whether from the accident or from him chewing it through, she couldn't be sure. She nudged him off her feet and flexed her toes, feet, ankles, and then her knees. No injuries—at least not that she could feel.

Just then a gust of wind blasted the side of her face, and she shivered. Where was *that* coming from? She turned, searching...and stared. The window in the passenger door was gone; jagged remnants were all that remained. The wind and snow were taking full advantage of the opening. Hence the little drifts of snow here and there in the cab.

"No wonder I'm so cold!"

Bo cocked his head, ears pricked, as though agreeing with her wholeheartedly. She lay her hand on the dog's broad head.

"I'm glad you're okay, boy, and that you're awake—" Emotion clutched at her throat, choking her. She pressed her forehead to the top of Bo's soft head. "It helps to have someone to talk to."

Bo rewarded her whispered admission with a quick lick. She rubbed his ears, then straightened, looking at the shattered window. "I've got to cover that up, boy. Which means I need to move."

This wasn't going to feel good. She forced her aching body into action, though the response was far slower than usual. Her fingers groped for the release on the seat belt, but it eluded her. Muttering her irritation, she shifted—then gasped at the pain that jabbed through her. She grabbed at her side, groaning, pressing her hands to her ribs. They must have been bruised by the seat belt when the truck hit bottom.

At least she hoped they were only bruised.

One thing was for sure, she needed more room to maneuver. She nudged Bo with her foot. "C'mon, boy, into the backseat." He resisted for a moment, then hopped across the wide console between the seats and moved to his blanket. He circled twice, three times, and then plopped down with a long-suffering grunt.

Renee inched her hand along the seat belt and fingered the catch, trying to stir up as little pain as possible. She let out a relieved breath when she pressed the release, and the seat belt snapped free. She pushed it aside and leaned toward Gabe, grimacing at the ugly gash on the side of his forehead. Blood trickled down his pale, still face.

Jesus...Jesus...

Even as the prayer escaped her frantic heart and flew skyward, her shaking increased. Blinding panic sparked to life somewhere deep in her gut, jumping and growing like flames in a stack of tinder-dry wood. Suddenly the cab felt as if it were closing in on her, and a chilling, wailing scream was filling her mind. She sat back, pressing her spine into the seatback, forcing herself to take deep, even breaths. With each puff of white as she exhaled, she repeated one fierce word: "Calm...calm...calm..."

She wasn't sure how long it took until her pulse resumed a more or less normal beat, but when it finally happened she sighed. If only she could stop shaking. It was partly nerves, partly the aching cold that seemed imbedded in her very bones.

And shock...it could be shock...

She pushed the grim thought aside, then swiveled to kneel on the seat and reach to the floor of the backseat. Amazingly, though he never took his eyes off her, Bo stayed where he was. She grabbed the strap of the canvas duffel bag with their clothes and supplies for their winter search-and-rescue training exercises. They'd joined the organization a few years ago, and though she enjoyed all she learned, Gabe had embraced it with unbridled enthusiasm. Search and Rescue was the perfect setting for his think-through-all-the-angles mindset.

As Renee tugged the bag toward her, she remembered her reaction when Gabe insisted they always needed to keep the search-and-rescue bag with them when they traveled in the winter. She had cast her gaze to the ceiling, making no effort to hide her disdain. He was, as usual, being overly cautious, hyper-vigilant. Why on earth couldn't the man just relax and have a good time?

Now...

She glanced at her unmoving husband and her throat caught. She swallowed back the wave of panic struggling to take over. *Steady, Renee. Don't fall apart now.* She looked at Bo. "Thank heaven he ignored me and listened to his instincts, eh, boy? He sure was right about this."

Bo's steady stare never wavered.

"I know, I know; it's too bad he isn't awake to hear me say that." She turned back to the bag. "Wouldn't he just love to hear me admit I was wrong."

Heaven knew he seldom heard those words from her. In fact, Renee thought, allowing herself a small smile, hearing her admit she was wrong might even make their nosedive down a mountain worthwhile. For Gabe, anyway.

She reached out to stroke the back of her husband's hand where it lay, so very still, on the console. "I'll tell you when you're conscious, Gabe. I promise."

Returning to her task, she tugged the bag until it landed in her lap. The increasing tremor in her hands made it a challenge to jerk the zipper open, but she finally succeeded. She pulled out gloves, a scarf, a hat, snowpants, each item making her feel like a giddy child on Christmas morning.

At the bottom of the bag were a blanket, an assortment of imperishables—chocolate bars, protein bars, dried fruit, nuts, water—and a large baggie with a dozen or so pocket heat packs. She cast another look at Gabe's still form. She'd told him those packs were probably just a way for the sporting goods stores to make money on people. But he pulled one out of the package and shook it, then handed it back to her. Amazingly, the tiny envelope generated serious heat.

Gabe had been the epitome of smugness as he took the

packet from her and flipped it in the air. "One of these little babies will last as long as twenty hours."

Twenty hours. God willing, they wouldn't need them for that long.

Her numb fingers fumbled with the extra clothing as she pulled the snowpants and a long-sleeved fleece top over her clothes. That done, she stuffed a few of the heat packs into her pockets, placing the rest back in the bag. As cold as it was now, when night fell it would only get colder. Better to save the heat packs until they really needed them.

Thankfully, warmth was coming back into her body. Remarkable what an extra layer of clothing could accomplish. With a fortifying breath, she reached under her seat for the small first-aid kit they stored there. Within minutes she had Gabe's wound cleaned and dressed, careful not to move his head in case there was any kind of neck injury. Relief whispered through her when she saw the bleeding on his forehead had stopped. As carefully as she could, she eased a knit cap over his thick hair.

Renee settled back in her seat, hugging herself. Now what? She glanced down at her purse and then, though she knew it was useless, reached down and pulled out her cell phone. Closing her eyes, she prayed for a miracle, then hit the power button. But when she opened her eyes what she saw on the LCD display was what she always saw on this section of road: No Service.

Teeth clenched, Renee tossed the phone back in her purse. She'd always teased Gabe that if they had trouble, it would probably happen on this stretch, where not even the booster antenna brought in a signal for their phones. "Just wait and see," she'd told him. "We'll be stuck in the middle of nowhere and have to hoof it for help."

For once, she wasn't the least bit happy about being right.

A blast of cold air and spitting snow hit her, and she took a quick look at her window, then at Bo. "I've got to find a way to block that wind, boy."

The tip of Bo's tail wagged. Obviously he agreed. Too bad he didn't have any ideas to offer. She peered into the backseat, then grabbed a ragged towel and Gabe's ever-present roll of gray tape.

"Duct tape," she heard his long-suffering voice correct her in her mind. He hated it when she called it gray tape, though she'd explained time and again that that was what her dad called it, so it only made sense she called it that as well. After all, the stuff was gray...

A scene flashed through her mind. She and Gabe couldn't have been married more than a few weeks when she'd first called it gray tape. He looked at her, eyes wide, mouth open, as though she just spit in his mother's soup or something equally unforgivable.

"It's called *duct* tape, Renee."

She wrinkled her nose, peering at the roll of tape in her hand. "Doesn't look like a duck to me."

He stared at her, then a wry smile lifted his lips. "Duct tape, with a *t*."

"Oh, of course, that makes so much more sense."

He had laughed then, and she joined him, throwing her arms around his waist and snuggling close. He looked down at her with such tenderness and ended the debate as he always did back then—back when things were so much simpler, so much easier to understand—by enfolding her in his arms and silencing her with a kiss.

Renee bit her lip. *We used to have so much fun...*

Shaking off the melancholy creeping over her, she turned to the window and got to work. It took longer than she liked to get it covered, but the band of pain that had taken up residence around her midsection wouldn't let her work more than a few seconds at a shot. When she finally finished, a thin sheen of perspiration was on her face. She was shaking again, and the thought she'd been avoiding forced its way into her mind.

Shock...I could be going into shock...

As though sensing her anxiety, Bo moved then, stretching out on top of the console and pressing his side into her. She leaned against him, grateful for the dog's warmth, and rubbed her hands up and down her arms, fighting her emotions. *Don't cry. It just makes it harder to breathe. Besides, you can't afford to lose the moisture.*

Renee gave a small laugh. None of this was the least bit funny, but she couldn't help it. That last thought had sounded so much like Gabe, in all his oh-so-practical glory. He was rubbing off on her, and for once, that was a good thing.

Pillowing her head on Bo's back, she looked at Gabe, then laid a hand on his shoulder, struggling to draw encouragement and strength from the steady rhythm of her husband's breathing.

And yet, as they lay there in the shrouded silence of the truck cab, she couldn't help but wonder, *Is this where it ends, Father?*

Autumn Dreams

by Gayle Roper
ISBN 1-59052-127-7, U.S. Suggested Retail Price: $11.99
350 pages, trade paperback, Fiction/General/Contemporary
Reader's Group Discussion Questions Available

May 2003

Cassandra Merton, newly forty and never married, is intrigued and intimidated by the rich forty-four-year-old bachelor who arrives at her Seaside, New Jersey, bed-and-breakfast. Management and finance specialist Dan Harmon is there to contemplate his life's significance as a result of witnessing the September 11 tragedy.

Meanwhile, Cass dares to resist being the family doormat for the first time in her life, as she struggles to care for her teenage niece and nephew as well as her aging, deteriorating parents. Strengthened by each other, the two baby boomers dedicate themselves to untangling life's puzzles—and a local mystery.

In writing *Autumn Dreams,* I drew heavily on our personal experiences with family. Like Cass we dealt with a mother slipping away from us long before she actually left. My favorite Mom story happened the day she looked at me and said, "I heard about you."

"Yeah? What did you hear, Mom?" I knew the answer would be very interesting.

"You're pregnant!" She grinned happily. I tried not to laugh.

"Mom, I'm too old." She looked at me in surprise, clearly convinced she was right and I was wrong. Fortunately, by our next visit, she had forgotten all about the pregnancy and told us about the trip she'd taken that morning to Washington state. The fact that she was wheelchair-bound in Pennsylvania meant nothing.

I enjoy hearing from my readers. Please stop by my website at www.gayleroper.com.

Gayle Roper

SAMPLE CHAPTER

Dan hurried downstairs, anxious to see Cass. He wanted to tell her about the opportunity to help Go and Tell International. It seemed to him that it was just the type of thing she'd be taken with. He was right.

"Oh, Dan, how wonderful that you can help here!" She blessed him with one of her glorious smiles. "Just think. You'll be helping with the spread of the gospel around the world. How special is that? If the Harmon Group were still going full-bore, you wouldn't have the time to give."

If the Harmon Group were still going, Dan thought, *I wouldn't be eating dinner with you.*

Jenn looked from Dan to Cass and back, and it was obvious that she was not impressed with Dan's opportunity. She looked at her brother, Jared. She took a couple of bites of her barbeque sandwich, then stood. "Call me when it's time to do the dishes. I'll be in my room. The company here is giving me a stomachache." Grabbing her plate and her drink, the teen clomped upstairs.

Jared watched her go, shaking his head. "I sure hope she grows up someday."

Dan very much agreed, thinking that she was like the hurricane that the weather service said was churning its way up the East Coast, all fury and flash, *Sturm und Drang.* He shoved a forkful of potato salad into his mouth to keep from saying so.

Cass placed a hand on Jared's as he reached for the bowl of fresh fruit. "Taking Paulie along on your double date wasn't the wisest thing you've ever done," she said gently. "You can't make her like him."

"At least Paulie's honorable." The depth of Jared's concern for his sister was clear to see, and Dan, already impressed with Jared's maturity, liked the boy even more. "I wouldn't have to worry about her with him. But Derrick—"

Cass released Jared's hand and patted it a couple of times. "I wish she liked Paulie too. Well, quite frankly, I wish she didn't like anyone. It would simplify all our lives. But if she's got to like anyone, I'd prefer Paulie over Derrick any day, too."

Since they were all in agreement on that issue, there seemed nothing more to say. They ate in silence for a minute. Then Cass spoke.

"Poor Dan. He's got this wonderful opportunity to serve the Lord, and what do we do? Get sidetracked. Tell us more about it, okay?"

"Yeah," Jared said, looking glad for the change of topic. "How come they got in trouble in the first place?"

"I don't know yet. That's part of what I'll have to find out." Dan eyed the platter of sloppy joes, debating with himself about taking another.

"Well, if money's a problem, they have to cut expenses somehow, don't they?" Jared took another roll full of hamburger barbeque, his third if Dan was counting correctly. "Isn't the best way to let people go? That's what they did at Dad's company a couple of years ago. They cut 10 percent of the workers across the board. Dad had to decide who in his department went. It almost gave him an ulcer."

Dan watched the boy devour his sandwich in four bites. Amazing. Had he taken time to chew, or did he just swallow it whole, sort of like a dog did? "Most people think you make cuts in a situation like GTI's, but I disagree. It's too easy to lose good workers that way. What you really need to do is increase income."

"But if they knew how to do that, they wouldn't be in this problem." Cass poured herself another glass of iced tea.

Dan held his glass out, and she filled it for him. He smiled his thanks. "My guess is that their problems aren't really financial, though that's what presents itself as obvious. The problems are more likely relational and psychological. By that I mean that they may have to get rid of some programs—and maybe some people—that they are attached to but are no longer doing the job they were designed or hired to do. Conversely, they may have to initiate some programs they've been loathe to establish. They may also have to hire some new highly qualified people."

"The old hire one, fire one," Cass said.

Dan looked at her in surprise.

"I might have been an English major, but I have a business minor. I've also taken several courses on running a B&B." She smiled sweetly and took a forkful of fruit salad. "I am not a dummy."

"No, you're anything but." Dan started to reach for the last sandwich and sighed as Jared beat him to it. That's what he got for hesitating.

When Cass called Jenn to come do the dishes, the girl came down with obvious reluctance, the great burden of unfair labor practices draped over her slim and undeserving shoulders. She did the dishes as noisily as she could manage.

Dan winced at every slap and slam of china and cutlery. The crash of the pans rattled the windows. "Are girls always like this when they're miffed?" he asked Cass *sotto voce* as the two of them lingered over their coffee.

"Just some girls. We happen to be living with a master."

Dan shook his head. Guys were so straightforward. If he'd had a gripe with his brother when they were young, he either pounded Andy into the ground or had it out verbally. "I never knew girls were so good at wringing every last dram of drama out of a situation."

"You poor sheltered man." Cass laughed softly at him.

"I bet you weren't like that when you were a kid, Cass." She was too straightforward to have ever been so. He knew it to his bones.

"I don't think I was. Neither my mother nor the brothers would have tolerated it. Besides, I'm a pleaser. Always have been."

He looked at her. She sure pleased him. "And she isn't?" He jerked his head toward the sink and Jenn as a particularly loud crash of pots sounded.

"Well, she doesn't like to purposely make people mad at her, but if things don't go as she likes, she's—" Cass searched for the right word.

"A pain in the neck?"

"Dan!" Cass said, but she was laughing.

Jenn turned to glare at them with a how-dare-you-be-happy-when-I'm-not stare.

Jared loped down the stairs and into the kitchen, a basketball tucked under his arm. "Hey, Dan, want to play some one-on-one?" He bounced the ball, making the whole room shudder. Jenn's glare intensified, something Dan found astounding. He wouldn't have thought she could look any angrier.

He looked at Cass. Much as he wanted the exercise and the challenge of beating the kid, he hated to abandon Cass to the irate Jenn. "Want to play too?"

She smiled. "Go ahead. I've got some things to plan for next week."

"You're sure?"

"Yes."

He nodded and turned to Jared. With a quick swipe, he stole the ball midbounce. He was just petty enough to enjoy the boy's startled look and Cass's admiring smile. At least he thought it was admiring. "Let's play, guy. I feel the need to whup someone."

"Yeah, right. Like you could." Jared grabbed the ball back and was out the door before Dan stood up.

Jared was good. He was quick on his feet, had a good eye, and had perfected a three-point shot that invariably slid through the hoop with barely a ripple of the net. When the kid learned not to whoop so loudly after each score, he'd be the consummate player.

"Do you play on your school team?" Dan asked, puffing more than he liked from chasing the kid all over the apron of Cass's drive.

Jared nodded as he feinted and drove for the basket. Only an inglorious lunge on Dan's part knocked the ball off its trajectory.

"Jared," Cass called from the back door. "Jeannie's on the phone for you."

The boy arched his eyebrows and grinned. Dan laughed as he retrieved the ball, dribbling it automatically.

"I'll only be a couple of minutes," Jared said as he passed Cass and went into the kitchen. He pulled the door closed behind him, leaving Cass on the outside.

She shook her head. "They're good for at least a half hour."

Dan agreed. "They've got last night and today to discuss."

Cass walked to the driveway and watched as he bounced the ball from hand to hand. After a minute, her hand lashed out and the ball was hers. She dribbled for the basket and jumped for as pretty a layup as he'd ever seen. She caught the ball as it dropped through the net, turned, and smiled at him in blatant challenge.

At first Dan checked himself as he played, not wanting to hurt her, but it soon became apparent that she had no similar qualms. She bumped him, elbowed him, and blocked him like she was one of the boys. His height and weight didn't intimidate her in the least.

"Four brothers," she said after throwing her hip and knocking him off-stride and out of bounds. The ball went flying. She reclaimed it with a grin and was at the basket before he was even back on the court.

From then on he played as if he were facing one of the guys. They both worked up a sweat, and Dan realized he hadn't had so much fun playing basketball in years. She wasn't as quick as Jared—twenty-two years was bound to slow someone—but she made up for any lacks in speed with skill and smarts. If he didn't stay on his toes, she'd beat him, something he had no doubt she'd love.

He scored, and she took the ball, dribbled to the back of the court, and began her move. She drove straight for him, feinted at the last second, and broke to her left. The first two times she'd tried that move, he fell for it. This time he was ready for her. She hit him hard, bounced off his chest, and started to go down. He grabbed for her, snaking an arm about her waist. She in turn clutched at his sweatshirt.

They ended up facing each other, mere inches apart. Somehow his second arm ended up around her, and he held her in a loose embrace. She felt good in his arms, substantial but definitely feminine. If he tightened his grip, he wouldn't have to worry about snapping her spine. If he kissed her, he wouldn't give himself a stiff back from bending low. She was just the right height, just the right size. Just the right person.

She looked up, startled to find herself held so close. He wasn't certain what he saw in his face, but her surprise vanished, replaced by a soft little smile that made his heart swell.

In the spotlight mounted on the corner of the garage, he could see little tendrils of hair, loosened from her ponytail by their vigorous game, curling around her lovely face. Her cheeks were rosy, and those wonderful eyes had a slightly dreamy look. Her breathing was accelerated. Just from the game? He knew his own heart was beating fast, and it wasn't all from exertion. Not by a long shot.

"You are so beautiful," he whispered.

She sighed, and the hands gripping his sweatshirt uncurled and slid to his shoulders. His arms wrapped more tightly about her. He leaned down and brushed her lips, his touch tentative. He hovered a moment, testing her reaction. He thought she leaned even closer. She definitely did not pull away.

Smiling inside, he kissed her again, a true kiss this time, one that stopped time, at least for him. At first she was hesitant, not pulling back, but not fully participating. Then suddenly her arms were around his neck and she kissed him back with an enthusiasm that matched his own.

When they finally pulled apart to take a much needed breath, he kept his arms tight so she wouldn't escape. When had he felt like this, kissing a woman, holding a woman? Had he ever reacted so strongly?

She laid her cheek against the hollow between his neck and shoulder, snuggled in, and took a few deep breaths. He smiled into her hair. He'd like nothing better than to kiss her again and again, but he knew he mustn't. It would be too much too quickly. Also, they were literally standing in the spotlight with Jenn and Jared mere feet away. Being a good example to them was important. And most important, as a Christian, he knew there had to be limits to physical expressions of affection, even the relatively safe and totally delightful action of kissing.

The back door slammed open, and Cass jumped like she'd been hit with a cattle prod. She pulled from him, eyes wide, looking like she was guilty of a terrible crime. He had to smile. All Jared had to do was look at his aunt, and he'd have a very good idea what she had been doing and with whom.

"I'm back," Jared announced as he grabbed the basketball, forgotten and lying at the edge of the drive. He dribbled to the basket and shot without looking at them. "Miss me?"

Cass almost ran to the door. "I-I'll just get back to my work."

Dan watched her go, and just before she pulled the back door shut behind her, she turned and looked at him. She gave a slight smile, then ducked her head and was gone.

He was still staring after her when the basketball hit him hard in the stomach. His air whooshed out, and he spun to Jared even as he rubbed his middle. What was the matter with the kid, throwing the ball that hard and without warning?

Jared stood, hands on hips, staring belligerently. "It's your turn."

It didn't take much to realize that Jared had seen the kisses and was feeling very protective of his aunt.

"I wouldn't hurt her for the world," Dan said, deciding to tackle the resentment head on.

Jared looked skeptical. "Do you love her? Are you going to marry her?"

Did he? Was he? Dan didn't know the answers to those questions yet. "I think she's marvelous. I like her immensely and enjoy her company."

"That's not what I asked."

"It's all I can tell you at the moment. I repeat, I won't hurt her."

"You're going to leave."

Dan sighed and nodded. He was, whenever God told him what He wanted from him, and implicit in his leaving was hurting Cass. He didn't even want to think about how much he might be hurt too.

"I don't think I want to play anymore tonight." Jared grabbed his basketball and headed for the house.

"I didn't force her to kiss me," Dan said. "And you're just afraid I'm going to whip the pants off you."

Jared froze. He turned slowly. "In your dreams. And all I want is her happiness."

Dan held his hands out for the ball. "On that we are agreed. And you just can't handle the idea of being beaten by an old man like me, can you?"

Jared's anger at Dan transmuted itself into aggressive play. In no time Dan's lungs burned as the boy raced around the court, and he was forced to follow. He also felt an interesting crop of bruises develop from Jared's very pointed elbows. When they stopped playing an hour later, Jared had trounced him soundly.

The good thing was that Jared had worked off his mad, and when they went into the kitchen and Dan suggested sharing the pitcher of iced tea, Jared joined him with all good humor.

❧

The bad thing was that Cass was nowhere to be seen.

At the sound of the alarm, Cass sat bolt upright in bed. Immediately she smelled smoke, lots of it. In the darkness of her little room, she couldn't see it, but she *felt* it in the heaviness of the air around her. Smoke. Terrible sulphur-smelling smoke! Fire!

Get out! Get out! Get the kids out. Grab Flossie and get out. Get Dan out.

She reached for the light on the tiny table by the bed. In her haste and fright, she knocked against the lamp, and it went tumbling over the far side of the table to crash in the tiny square of space between the bureau and the wall. Even over the blare of the alarm she heard the pop as the bulb shattered.

In blackness she slid from bed onto the narrow alley of floor, barely registering the chill in the November air. She knew she had to be low to stay under the worst of the fumes, to find air that was safe to breathe. Keeping her head down, she reached up, feeling for Flossie who lay sleeping somewhere in the blankets, oblivious of the bleating alarm. Cass had thought the animal was going deaf, but now she knew for certain. No creature with working ears could miss the cacophony of the alarm.

She felt all over the comforter without finding Flossie. She took a deep breath, rose up on her knees, and threw the comforter over the foot of the bed, no easy task in her position. She skimmed the blanket with her hands. No Flossie. She threw it back too and felt wildly about. She was running out of air and time. Her hand smacked into a pile of warm fur that grunted at the slug she'd inadvertently given it. Cass grabbed the startled cat, tucked her under one arm, and dropped back to all fours to crawl out of the room.

She'd taken no more than two steps when the door to her room burst open. Dan rushed in, bringing very dim light from the kitchen and setting the thick smoke to swirling wildly in the new air currents.

"Cass! Cass!" he yelled, then tripped over the foot of the bed. With a yelp of pain he sprawled full length where a minute or two before she had slept.

She could hear Jenn and Jared calling her name from the smoke-shrouded kitchen. She yelled, "I'm coming! Go outside! Go!"

"Cass!" Dan was flailing around in the bed, searching for her, and she realized he couldn't see her down on the floor.

"I'm here," she shouted over the bleat of the alarm, reaching up and slapping at the bed. She connected with his leg, stinging her hand.

Dan growled something and rolled off the empty bed, knocking her back down again. As his weight hit her, she collapsed facedown in the tiny space between the bed and the dresser, catching one of the dresser knobs as she fell. Pain.

Flossie, caught beneath Cass, let out a fierce howl at the indignity of being squashed and began to claw her way free. The animal only had her rear claws, but her desperation made them more than enough.

"Ouch, ouch, ouch!" Cass yelled as fiery scratches burned down her arm. She managed to lift her upper body enough to free the cat who streaked from the room. She collapsed immediately as Dan fell into her, trying to turn toward the door in a space not meant for anyone his size to move.

"Out!" Dan swatted at her.

"Off," Cass gasped, elbowing him in the solar plexus.

Dan groaned and shifted to the side as much as he could, which wasn't much. "Just get out," he yelled. "The smoke is gathering in here." He coughed, a deep,

ugly rasp and scrambled to turn himself around, kicking her a couple of times in the process.

Cass pulled herself forward on her elbows like a soldier under fire. When she was free from the bulk of his weight, she got back to her knees and began crawling. Her head spun, her lungs burned with the effects of the smoke, and her stomach heaved at the noxious rotten egg smell.

"Hurry." Dan's hand found her leg and pushed. He coughed some more.

Cass crawled into and across the kitchen and out the door the kids had left open behind them. Once outside she got to her feet and headed for the sycamore. The clean cold air washed over her. Sinking to her knees, she pressed her hands to her aching chest and breathed it in. Wonderful!

"I called 911," Jenn said, holding her cell phone in Cass's face. "I called them as soon as I got outside."

Cass looked up at Jenn who had on a fuzzy blue robe and white bunny slippers.

"Good girl. Thanks, Jenn." She reached out and patted a bunny slipper. But was a cell phone the first thing to grab in case of fire?

Beside her, still on his hands and knees, Dan inhaled and coughed, inhaled and coughed.

"Are you okay?" She laid her hand on his back as, head down, he struggled for breath.

"Yeah, I'm fine." His voice was raspy, but he was obviously breathing more easily all the time. He turned and sat, leaning his back against the tree. She turned and propped herself against the tree beside him. They stared at the house as they waited for the fire engines.

Poor firemen, Cass thought. All volunteers, pulled out of bed in the middle of the night.

"Where's the fire?" Jared asked after a few minutes. "There's no fire."

"What do you mean?" Cass stared at SeaSong. Jared was right as far as she could see. "But all the smoke—"It poured out the back door and out the window over the kitchen sink.

Jared, wearing only old sweatpants that looked as if they'd lost all their elastic or their drawstring and threatened to slip off his narrow hips at any minute, walked to one side of the house and then the other. "Something's weird here." He disappeared down the side yard.

"Be careful!" Cass called after him. She shivered as a gust of wind whipped by. She wrapped her arms about herself in a futile attempt to keep warm. She wanted the throw that Paulie had brought for Mom. She looked down at her *She sells seashells by the Seaside* night shirt and shivered again. If it wouldn't keep her warm in bed under the covers unless the cat cuddled against her, there wasn't a ghost of a chance it'd do much good out here. At least she had her heavy socks on. Poor Dan's bare feet must be freezing. He sat beside her dressed in a T-shirt and jeans.

Cass shivered again, and Dan slid his arm around her shoulders. "Lean in. We'll keep each other warm."

Cass leaned, angling so her back rested against part of Dan's chest. Immediately his body heat eased her shivering. He rested his cheek against Cass's head, and she closed her eyes to enjoy his nearness.

"I'm just glad there aren't any other guests," she said, thinking of the chaos and danger if there had been. "And thank goodness the insurance is paid."

Dan's arm tightened about her. "Don't ever do that to me again," he said softly. "You scared me to death." His voice was rough.

She turned and looked back at him, but she couldn't see his face with it buried in her hair. "Do what?"

"The kids were both out in the yard when I hit the kitchen, but you weren't anywhere in sight. All that smoke, so dense in the kitchen, and your closed door. I thought my heart would stop."

"Yeah?" Sorry as she was that he'd been worried, she definitely felt toasty at that revelation. "And that's when you crashed into my room?"

"That's when I came to save you," he corrected, kissing the top of her head.

Jared reappeared on the far side of the house. "Still no fire. And there's only smoke in the back. Could be the way the wind's blowing or something. I went up on the front porch and peered in the door and windows. No smoke."

Dan hauled himself to his feet, and Cass felt the loss of his heat immediately. Sighing, she climbed to her feet too. She could hear the sirens drawing closer by the second.

"You're right, Jared," Dan said. "Now that I'm thinking more clearly, there was no smoke until I pushed the door open to the kitchen. Then there was plenty, and it smelled like rotten eggs."

"Reminds me of a chemistry experiment gone bad," Jared said.

Cass studied SeaSong. Jared and Dan were right.

Something was weird here.

Jared pointed. "How'd the kitchen window get broken? Did any of you break it?"

Cass, Jenn, and Dan shook their heads as they followed Jared and stood staring at the kitchen window, or rather the place where the window had been. All that remained of the lower sash were a few shards sticking out at varying angles like transparent knives.

"Maybe the heat from the fire blew it out?" Cass suggested.

"What heat?" Dan shuddered with the cold. "There's no heat, just like there's no flames." He started toward the kitchen door.

Cass grabbed his arm. "Where are you going?"

"If there's no heat and no flames, there's no fire. I want to see what's going on."

"Yeah, me too." Jared was excited, ready to race into the house with Dan.

Cass grabbed Jared with her other hand. She glared at them both. "Let the firemen go in first! They're almost here."

Even as she spoke, Sheriff Greg Barnes pulled up to SeaSong for the second time that night. The fire department was right on his bumper. Men in their heavy coats, boots and hats filled the yard. One shooed Cass, Dan, and the kids back out of their way. Others grabbed the hoses and attached them to the nearby hydrant. Neighbors who began appearing at the sound of the blaring alarm gathered in little groups, whispering among themselves. All the commotion almost drowned out the still bleating alarm.

Reminder: Thank the company that had hardwired the system through the whole house for her. It worked very well.

Cass looked at the heavy hoses and imagined the

destruction to SeaSong under the pressure of the water that would explode as soon as the nozzles were opened.

"Wait!" she cried, rushing up to the first man on the hose. "We don't think there's a fire. See?" She waved her hand at the house. "No flames. Please don't make water damage! I've got irreplaceable antiques in there."

"Lady," the fireman said politely, "if we don't find fire, we won't shoot water. I promise."

Feeling like an idiot but still glad she'd spoken, Cass stood with Dan and the kids and watched as the firemen swarmed in and out of SeaSong.

"You were right," Greg told them after conferring with the fire chief. "There's no sign of fire. Just the remains of a smoke bomb in the sink."

"A smoke bomb in the sink?" Cass could hardly believe her ears. "Are you sure?"

"The paper lying in the sink is clearly the remains of the wrappings of a spent smoke bomb. We all recognized it right away because we use bombs like that in training drills. Someone broke the window and dropped the lit bomb in the sink."

"But why?" Cass stared at the broken window where wisps of white smoke still appeared.

"Random malicious mischief," Greg offered. "That's our best guess. That is, unless you've got a secret enemy out there trying to harm you." He smiled at the absurdity of that idea.

Enemies? Her? Cass shook her head, bewildered. "It makes no sense."

Greg shrugged. "This kind of vandalism rarely does."

"You mentioned an enemy harming her. How would the smoke bomb harm her?" Dan asked. "Aside from scaring us all and forcing us out into the night."

"The smell," Greg said. "It could drive away the guests at a B&B easily."

"But I don't have any guests but Dan." Cass shivered and not just from the cold. *An enemy?*

"We'll do our best to find those responsible," Greg said, "but hit-and-run nastiness like this is hard to trace." He patted Cass awkwardly on the shoulder.

And that's supposed to make me feel better? Cass wanted to ask but didn't. She was afraid she was feeling more than a bit whiny, but then she'd never had her personal space invaded in such an act of vandalism before.

She rubbed her arms, trying to get the goose bumps to go away. SeaSong, the castle she'd built by the sea, had been breached.

Antonia's Choice

by Nancy Rue
ISBN 1-59052-076-9, U.S. Suggested Retail Price: $11.99
300 pages, trade paperback, Fiction/General/Contemporary
Reader's Group Discfussion Questions Available

May 2003

When career woman Toni Wells discovers that her
five-year-old has been molested by a child pornogra-
pher, she must finally choose between maintaining
her own lifestyle and helping her son recover.

Antonia's Choice was written for anyone who has
ever had to make a decision that cost her, which
would include just about every woman I know! For
Toni Wells, the main character in the novel, the

choices she has to make cost her everything. Everything.

All of the things she has always thought vital to her happiness are called into question when Toni finds out that her five-year-old son has been the victim of pornography, at the hands of her own brother-in-law. Although that explains her little boy's recent bizarre behavior, it also forces her to make a series of choices in which she can't stop to count the cost of making the only decision she can.

Her choices are painful and they leave her reeling—and they nurture growth in her as nothing else has. This is a book about redemption and renewal, about rebirth and reconciliation. Yes, it will grieve you with its sensitively presented picture of the all-too-prevalent sexual abuse of children, but it will also give you the same hope that Toni embraces—the hope we have when we surrender it all to God and start from there.

Nancy Rue

SAMPLE CHAPTER

"All right," I called out from the front door. "If we don't *run* to the car, we aren't going to get there. Ben, where are you?"

My son didn't show himself. Only his husky voice made its hoarse little way out from behind one of the living room columns.

"I'm not gonna run. I hate running."

"That doesn't surprise me," I said. "Tell me something you *don't* 'hate' this morning. *That* will surprise me."

"I hate—"

"Don't say *hate,* Ben," Stephanie said. "I hate that."

My sister stopped rolling her suitcase across the foyer's fieldstone floor and lured Ben out from behind the column by the hand. Her dark eyes danced down at him. "What are you hating this morning, buddy? Tell Aunt Stephanie all about it."

"Thank you, Steph," I said dryly. "You're so helpful."

"You're going to miss me and you know it," she said to me. Then she squatted down to meet the small, inquisitive face at eye level. "Come on, Ben. Dish, dude."

I didn't comment that it was no wonder Ben's vocabulary had gone completely down the tubes the last two weeks. Between Stephanie's twenty-seven-year-old slang and my mother's grandmotherly toddler-talk, it was amazing my usually precocious kindergartner could even put a complete sentence together now. But I just shooed both of them toward the front door. At least Stephanie had gotten the scowl off Ben's face. It was more than I could say for my own ability lately.

"Mama!" I called out over my shoulder. "Let's shake a leg."

It was a pointless request, of course. My classy mother never "shook" anything. It was customary for her to float, as she did now, down the steps into the foyer, one set of manicured nails resting lightly on the cherry stair rail while the other balanced a leather bag on her shoulder.

Every pristine white hair of her fashionable bob was in place, and English Toffee lipstick was drawn on without a hint of feathering into the tiny age wrinkles that fringed her lips. Silk sleeves fell down her arms in cascading folds. I knew she was aware that she was in danger of missing her plane, but the passing stranger would have thought she was making an entrance for a leisurely brunch.

And there I was, shoving my hair behind my ears, wearing wrinkles into my linen pants, and, at only 7:30 A.M., already wishing I'd worn flats instead of pumps.

"Mama," I said with forced patience, "we have to drop Ben off at school before I take you to the airport. You're going to need to step it up a little."

"I was just leaving you a little something upstairs," Mama said. She didn't "step it up" by so much as a millisecond.

"You didn't have to do that—"

"If I didn't, there would be no end to the whining about your being the neglected middle child."

"I don't whine!" I took the bag from her and headed for the door. "Thirty-seven-year-old women do not whine."

"Children always whine to their mothers, no matter how old they get."

I looked out at Ben, who was climbing into the Lexus under Stephanie's supervision. "Wonderful," I said.

For the moment, Ben was being cooperative, settling himself into the booster seat that had recently replaced his car seat and letting Stephanie help him buckle the belt. I knew the minute he saw me in the vicinity, he'd start wailing about something—anything.

I charged toward the trunk with my mother's bag, my head spinning once again into the day that lay ahead of me. I had to get Ben to school on time, or he wasn't going to get the perfect attendance award, and he'd be wailing about that longer than I could listen to him.

According to the new regulations, Mama and Stephanie had to be at the airport two hours before their flight left, despite the fact that they were only flying from Nashville to Richmond. They'd probably stand in line at the security checkpoint longer than they'd be in the air. And then I had at least a ten-hour day at the office ahead of me, unless I brought files home to work on after Ben went to bed.

I slammed the trunk and looked at the back of Ben's dark head through the rear window. At the moment, he was rattling something off to Stephanie, his head bobbing, the crown hair I'd wet down so carefully—under protest—sticking straight up like a paintbrush.

It had taken two hours to get him to sleep the night before, and once he finally drifted off, he was awake two hours later in a wet bed. That happened at least five nights out of seven, so the chances of me actually getting any work done at home in the evenings were slim to none. But I was going to have to. If I continued to stay at the office until I was caught up, Ben would be home with Lindsay, the after-school babysitter, into the evening, which would lead to its own share of crying and carrying on once I came on the scene.

I slid into the front seat and started up the car. When I wasn't with Ben at home, he pitched fits. When I was with him, he pitched fits. The child pitched fits when he was asleep. I was ready to pitch one myself. Hence the plan I was going to present to Jeffrey Faustman this morning.

"I'm giving this posh neighborhood one last look," Steph said from the backseat as I pulled out of Belle Meade, "before I go back to my stinky little apartment."

"Stephanie Lynn," my mother said, "your apartment is darling." She looked at me pointedly. "You haven't seen it, have you?"

"No," I said, fighting the urge to remind my mother that she had asked me that at least fourteen times over the last two weeks.

"You aren't missing that much, Toni," Stephanie said. "Just think about my room at college, spread it over a living room, a kitchen, and a bedroom, and you've got my apartment."

"That bad, huh?" I gave my little sister a grateful look in the rearview mirror. Fair or not, it was her job in the family to keep conversations from taking dead-end turns. She'd been working pretty hard at it during their stay. I suspected she'd go home to her "stinky little apartment" and collapse.

"Am I gonna be late?" Ben said.

"No," I said. "Do I ever get you there late?"

"Almost."

"Almost doesn't count."

"Other kids get there *way* early."

"So—you're here a *little* early." I swung into the tunnel of about-to-blossom dogwood trees that arched the driveway of Hillsboro Private School and snapped my seat belt open. "It's the best I can do, pal."

Ben squirmed out of his booster seat, his face puckering as he eyed the front door. "I'm late. I can feel it."

"Did you give Aunt Stephanie and Nana a kiss?" I said. "You aren't going to see them for a while."

Ben's attention immediately shifted to his grandmother's face, and I groaned inwardly. His honey-brown eyes were narrowing into accusatory pinpoints.

"Why?" he said. "Why aren't I seeing them for a while?"

"We have to go home, buddy," Stephanie said.

"Why?"

"Because I have to go to work."

"No!"

"Ben, I have to take them to the airport," I said, pulling gently at his sleeve. "You'll see them again."

"When?"

"Soon." My mother leaned over the backseat and tilted Ben's chin up with her fingers. "You remember what we talked about."

Ben nodded sullenly.

"You'll see us before you know it—and for a long time."

"But I don't want—"

"Let's go, pal." I gave the sleeve another tug, which was obviously one tug too many.

Ben snatched himself away from me, both elbows swinging. "I don't wanna go to school! I hate school!"

"You do not," I said. "You love school. Kiss Aunt Stephanie good-bye. They have to go."

"No! I hate Aunt Stephanie!"

"Benjamin!" I said.

"Love you, too, buddy," Stephanie said.

Ben didn't appear to hear her as he struggled under my hands, which were dragging him onto the sidewalk. He wrenched himself away from me and stood, arms folded across his narrow little chest, gaze hard on the ground.

"You know you're going to be fine as soon as you get in there," I said. "So I don't see why we need to go through this every day. Here's your backpack."

I produced the Power Rangers pack, stuffed with lunch and crayons and an odd assortment of accessories Ben couldn't live without. He smacked it out of my hand and refolded his arms. It was all I could do to squat in front of him, rather than jerk him up by the arm and haul his little backside up to the front door.

"If I knew why all of a sudden you don't want to go to school anymore, I could help you," I said. "But since you can't tell me, all I can do is get you here." My eyes narrowed as I went for his little mental jugular. "But if you don't go inside, you aren't going to get the perfect attendance award, because you're going to be late."

The arms sprang away from his body like surprised springs, and he snatched for the backpack.

"You made me late!" he shouted—for every Belle Meade mother in the parking lot to hear. "I hate you!"

I'd heard those three words countless times over the last several months, but I still felt as if I'd been shot every time they came out of his mouth. I even put my hand flat against my chest as I watched his lanky little figure tear up the sidewalk for the door. What had happened to the precious little preschool chunkiness—and the so-alive eyes—and the sweet, chirped-out words "I love you"?

As I climbed back into the Lexus, I hoped my mother and Stephanie hadn't heard Ben's parting shot, but the distress etched into Mama's face dashed that to the dust.

"He's just upset because we're leaving," Stephanie said

even before I got the car into reverse.

"There's a lot more to it than that," Mama said. "And, Toni, you know it."

I gritted my teeth, overbite and all. Somehow we had made it through two weeks without getting into this. There we were on our way to the airport, and she had to start in. We only had to get to I-40, and we'd practically be at the terminal. If I wanted to get a word in myself, I was going to have to cut right to the chase. "You're thinking that if Chris and I weren't separated, Ben wouldn't be acting this way."

Mama's eyes sprang open a little. "That's exactly what I'm saying. And I think it's worse because you've moved him five hundred miles from his father so he barely gets to see the man."

"Chris was just here the week before you came. They went to Disneyworld."

"It was a vacation," Mom said. "That doesn't constitute a relationship between a father and a son."

"It's something, though," Stephanie said. "I think Toni's doing the best she can—"

"Chris should've thought about his relationship with his son before he slept with another woman," I said. I'd already hit I-40. I had to move on.

"For heaven's sake, Antonia," my mother said. "Can't you forgive the man one transgression? It's not as if he was a drunk or into drugs—something he was refusing to change. Chris isn't going to make that mistake again."

I took my eyes off the Mercedes in front of me long enough to give her a look. "How could you possibly know that? *I* don't know it. I don't know that I can trust Chris now. He did it once—why wouldn't he do it again?"

"Because you would work on your marriage. But you

won't even try. You refuse to go to counseling—"

"I don't believe in letting some third party who has no idea what I've been through tell me what to do."

I gunned the motor and slipped in front of a semi in the right lane. Maybe it was a good thing that most of the heavy traffic on I-40 was headed into Nashville while we headed out. This trip couldn't be fast enough at this point. As I checked to make sure the trucker I'd just cut off wasn't going to rear-end me, I caught Stephanie's face in the rearview mirror.

She was sucking in her bottom lip, accentuating the Kerrington overbite. A tiny line had appeared between her wide eyes, and she was toying with one of the dark curls that fell over her shoulder.

Even as the angst built in her face, I still thought she was the prettiest of us three girls, inheriting our father's handsomeness in a way I could never hope to. It wasn't just the to-die-for hair, the willowy figure, the big eyes. It was the compassion that came out of every pore—and had me spilling my guts to her every time I got the chance. She knew, because I had told her, that there was more to my split with Chris than his affair. And she knew I didn't want to go there with Mama—who since our father's death five years ago had begun to deify marriage.

Besides, I didn't even want to go there with myself right now. My back was doing that thing it did every time I thought about Chris. It stiffened from the base of my spine to the back of my head, and my jaws tightened down as if Chris himself were in there with a ratchet set. I was going to be in pain any second if I didn't manipulate a subject change.

"Children need to be with their parents—both their parents," Mama said.

"Are you going to start comparing me to Bobbi?" I said. It

was a pretty weak segue, but it was the best I could do on the spot.

"I never compare you girls to each other. But since you brought it up, Bobbi and Sid are both with their children, yes."

"And your point is?" I said. "Every time I've seen them over the last two years, they looked like a pretty miserable little group to me. Sid moping over in the corner. Bobbi with the two little ones hanging on her like baby monkeys with their noses running." I put up my hand. "No, make that Emil still breast feeding at age three and a half, and Techla hanging on Wyndham—who to me is more like a nanny than a teenage girl. Yeah, being together as a family is really working for them."

"You haven't seen them since you moved," Mama said. "What's that, two and a half months now?"

I didn't answer.

"They're actually doing better," Stephanie said. "I mean, at least it seemed like it Valentine's Day when I went over to take the kids their presents."

"They were in financial trouble over the past few years, you know that," Mama said. "Something like that can bring a family down. But the point is that they stayed together and toughed it out, and I think they're stronger for it."

I exchanged glances with Stephanie in the mirror. Her eye roll reflected my own disgust with Mama's always-predictable defense of Bobbi. Our older sister could rob a bank and Mama would find a way to make it a virtuous deed on Bobbi's part. *"She's always been fragile,"* Mama had said approximately a thousand times. *"Her sensitivity is what makes her such a beautiful person."*

I loved my sister because…she was my sister. But in my view, Bobbi had always been a wimp. Her neediness was what made her such a pain to be around for more than thirty minutes.

Besides, she didn't really need me when she'd had Mama fawning over her all her life.

I could feel my mother giving me a pointed look. "I think it helped that Bobbi is a stay-at-home mom."

"It might help Sid," I said, "but I don't think it helps Bobbi. Personally, I think it would do her good to get her focus off the kids and him for at least a couple of hours a day."

My mother chewed on that for a second before she said, "Bobbi's services as a babysitter certainly came in handy for you during those last months before you left Richmond."

"I didn't leave Ben there because I needed a babysitter," I said tightly. "Ben loves Emil. They're more like twins than Emil and Techla are. Ben was having a rough time, and I thought it was good for him to be with his cousin."

"No need to get defensive," Mom said. "I was just pointing out that—"

"So what's Sid doing now?" I didn't really care what my brother-in-law did. He'd never been my favorite human being; he just came in handy at the moment.

"Something with computers," Mom said.

"I thought he lost his shirt in that dot-com thing he was involved in."

"This is different—he's doing something with websites, and it's obviously very successful."

"Ya think?" Stephanie said. "They just added a whole studio onto their house."

"That place was four thousand square feet to begin with."

Stephanie gave one of her signature snorts. "You don't exactly live in a shack yourself."

"My shack's rented," I said. "And I can only afford that because it belongs to a client."

"There's nothing wrong with the house you and Chris *own* in Richmond, either," Mama said. "I drive by it every now and then. Chris is keeping the lawn up."

I had never been so glad to see the Nashville terminal, or more grateful for the overzealous security people who blew their whistles if a driver left his car stopped at the curb for more than seven seconds.

"I would come in with you," I said, flipping the trunk release and whipping open my door, "but I really have to get to work."

"Not a problem," Stephanie said. She caught up with me at the trunk and planted a kiss on my cheek.

I felt a wave of longing. I really wanted her to stay.

My mother pulled me into her arms then, and I felt just as overwhelming a wave—of guilt. She really cared. I knew that. And I could be such a witch in the face of it.

Spine feeling like a piece of barbed wire, I hugged her back and whispered that I loved her. Mama's face looked pained as the guard blew insistently on his whistle and she pulled away.

"I love you, too. And I just want you to be happy. I know that if you would just—"

"Come on, Mama, before this poor man blows a gasket," Stephanie said. "Love you, Sis."

I blew them both a kiss and slid back into the front seat, cupping myself in leather. It was suddenly too quiet in the car. All the stuff Mama had just opened up about Chris and about Ben filled up the air space.

"I'm not going there," I said out loud. "Work. Think about work."

Not hard to do. I had the meeting with Jeffrey first thing that I needed to concentrate on.

As I waited behind a line of cars, I glanced in the rearview mirror again to make sure I had the right look for the meeting. Aside from the tousled hair, the result of having done a whole day's work already, I was probably passable.

That sent a pang through me. Chris had always said that. I would come out of the bedroom after an hour in front of the mirror and he'd get that impish glimmer in his eyes and smile—his smile was so slow it was maddening—and he'd say, "You'll pass."

In his more amorous moments, of course, it had been different. The Louisiana drawl he'd tried so hard to hide since law school would ooze right on out into, "Baby, do you know how hard it was for me to keep my hands out of your hair this entire evening?"

"I'm so sure you were going to run your fingers through my hair while you were entertaining clients, Wells," I would tell him. "Give me a break."

"I'm serious, darlin'. I saw it all thick and blond and tucked behind your ears, and I wanted to slide my fingers right in there."

"Get over yourself!"

"Look at your eyes, lookin' so brown, just a-twinklin' at me, telling me, 'Come here, boy.'"

"In your dreams."

"Let me just hug on that cute little ol' body—"

Uh-huh, I thought now. *Did you say the same things to that little paralegal you bedded down?*

I shook my head, tossing back my bangs. *Don't go there. Do not EVEN go there.*

I went back to Jeffrey Faustman.

Whether or not my mother was right about the causes of

Ben's behavior, it was obvious I was going to have to do something about it before he started slipping out at night with a can of spray paint. Not to mention the fact that Ben and I were miserable. It seemed like all we did was scream at each other. Chris and I hadn't even done that, which made me wonder why Ben had chosen that as his latest means of expressing himself.

During the two weeks my mother was there I had had to admit, begrudgingly, that she was correct about one thing: I wasn't spending enough time with Ben. An hour in the morning, trying to get cereal down his throat without tossing the whole bowl against the wall, and an hour and a half between the time I got home from work and the time he was supposed to be in bed really didn't cut it.

The night before, when I'd finally gotten Ben to sleep for the second time after the bed-wetting ordeal, I'd stayed up forming a plan, which by dawn sounded reasonable to me. Now I just had to convince Jeffrey.

The baggy-pants gardener was out in front of Faustman Financial Services putting in a flat of pansies when I pulled into the circular driveway. For a mad moment I wished I had his job, complete with the amount of derriere he was showing over the top of his rather pointless belt. To my knowledge he never had to take files home.

You know you love what you do, I told myself. You'll get through this phase with Ben, and then you can get refocused on the joys of handling other people's money. You can do this. You can do anything.

I could feel myself setting my jaw, bringing my overbite into full view. As vain as I admittedly was about my appearance, I'd never wanted to have that fixed. I'd seen myself once when a TV camera had caught me cheering in the Orange Bowl, the year Florida was ranked number one, and I'd kind of liked the overbite. It gave me character. Chris always said so.

"Would you *stop!*" I said into the rearview. "What is with the Chris obsession today?"

I marched my little self up to the oak double doors and breezed into the foyer, where the brass umbrella stand and the leaf-perfect ficus plant greeted me. Regina Acklee looked up from the reception desk, blue eyes taking inventory.

"You on a mission this mornin', honey?" she said. She glanced at the grandfather clock that ticked solemnly across from her desk. "Jeffrey's gonna wish your mission was to get here on time."

"What am I, two minutes late?" I said.

"Ninety seconds." She gave me a toothy smile. "But who's counting?"

I set my briefcase down on the marble floor and sat on the edge of the chair at Reggie's desk. I could feel the bumps of the brocade through my pants.

"What kind of mood is he in?"

Reggie glanced over both shoulders at the office, which was perfectly quiet except for the soft tinkle of Mozart. If anyone were blinking within a hundred feet, we would have heard it.

Reggie then leaned forward, fingernails tapping on the oak desktop. I couldn't resist a peek at what she had going today. One shade short of fire engine red, each with a slant of gold. The pinkie had a ring in it. I could never figure out how she typed with those talons.

"He's Mr. Business today," she said, barely moving her lips. "You know, all crisp—callin' me Miz Acklee and tellin' me to hold his calls."

"Oh."

Her eyes narrowed, revealing more of the makeup job that must take her two hours to apply with that kind of precision. I'd always been in awe of it.

"What kind of mission are you on, honey?"

Although I was an associate and Reggie was the receptionist, it had never bothered me that she called me "honey," "baby," "sugar," and assorted combinations thereof. I trusted her more than I did anyone else in the office, including my own assistant, who daily made it evident that it was my job she'd really rather have.

Reggie was watching me closely. "The way you're lookin'," she said, "this may not be the day to approach His Worshipfulness."

"I have to. I've got to spend more time with Ben, so I'm going to ask Jeffrey to let me work mornings here and afternoons at home. I can schedule all my appointments in the mornings, and if I have to do any evening meetings I can get a babysitter and do them after Ben goes to sleep. *If* he goes to sleep."

"Oh, honey, does he still have that screamin' thing goin' on?"

I nodded. "But I'm thinking that if I spend more time with him—maybe get him into some sports activities to burn up some of that energy—he'll start to settle down some. Don't they have soccer and baseball for kindergarten-age kids?"

"Are you kiddin', baby? Every child in Davidson County is on a soccer or T-ball team the minute he leaves the playpen."

"Then Ben's behind." I cocked my head at her. "And what's T-ball?"

"Oh, honey, you have got a lot to learn." She shook her head, wagging the strawberry-blond ponytail. She was the only nearly-forty-year-old woman I knew who could still get away with a ponytail at the office. And if Jeffrey had disapproved, he would have told her so long ago.

She was blinking at me now.

"What?" I said.

"I'm just thinkin'—and mind you, this is just my intuition—but I'm just thinkin' Jeffrey is *not* gonna go for that plan at *all*. Not the way he's acting this mornin'. First thing he did when he came in here was check to make sure everybody's desk was left neat last night."

"Why—so the cleaning crew would be impressed?" I said.

"All I'm sayin' is that if you could put it off till another day, you might have a better chance."

"I can't wait. Either Ben's going to pop a blood vessel or I'm going to haul off and smack him."

Reggie nodded, her very-round face soft. "I'm so sorry ya'll are goin' through this. I'm prayin' for you."

"Thanks," I said automatically.

Reggie was always reassuring me of her ongoing prayers, and I didn't have a problem with that. I'd been brought up with Sunday school and potluck suppers and mite boxes during Lent. But right now I just didn't see what good praying was going to do. Even God, I was sure, couldn't loosen Jeffrey up. That was going to be up to me.

I dropped off my briefcase and purse in my office, giving a list for the day to Ginny, my assistant, who greeted it with the usual poorly disguised lip curl. After stopping by the restroom for one last perusal in the mirror, I headed for Jeffrey's office. My pants were so wrinkled in the front they looked like an accordion, but otherwise I had the confident, professional look going on. It was all about attitude.

The oak door with its JEFFREY R. FAUSTMAN, JR. brass plate was closed when I got there. I knocked soundly and pushed it open. I hadn't called first and I didn't wait for an invitation to come in. Where I was headed, it was better not to give Faustman opportunities to say no to anything along the way.

Jeffrey's bald head, still bent over the desk as I stepped into his office, caught the carefully focused track lighting. I'd often wondered how he achieved the perfect shine on the completely hairless part of his head. It was as flawless as the thick fringe of auburn below it. I'd always meant to ask Reggie if she thought he waxed his cranium.

When he looked up, I caught the fleeting irritation behind his glasses, but as soon as he stood up it was gone. Jeffrey Faustman never lowered himself to emotion. With the clients he was cordial and showed an understated charm. Ours were the kind of clients who had been schmoozed over enough to be able to spot it the minute they crossed the threshold, and would turn on their heels to avoid it. With the staff, on Reggie's level, he was crisp and businesslike, bordering on abrupt, at times resorting to rude. With his associates, like myself, he was professional and polite, drawn into our personal concerns only on rare occasions. As I settled back into the Queen Anne chair in front of his desk, I was determined this wasn't going to be one of those occasions.

"Were we scheduled to meet this morning?" he said, glancing at his Day-Timer as he returned to his desk chair. He looked six-foot-three when he sat, or when he was standing over someone's desk, but he was barely six feet tall. I drew myself up as far as my own five-foot-four self would allow.

"No," I said. "But there's something I need to discuss with you before the day gets going."

"Mine is already going."

There were lifted eyebrows, which I ignored.

"I'm going to need to change my working arrangement. The details are outlined here."

I slid a file across his desk and leaned back against the silk brocade while he glanced over my plan. I had purposely not referred to it as a "proposal."

He closed the file and lined it up precisely on his desktop. "What's this about, Toni?"

"It's about my needing to change my working hours."

"Why?"

"It's personal."

"I don't think I'm overstepping my boundaries by asking you for details."

He wasn't. I had to answer.

"My circumstances have changed," I said.

"Are you getting back together with your husband?"

"No!" I said, and then silently cursed myself. Bad move. Regroup. "No," I said, minus the exclamation point. "It's nothing like that. My son just needs more of my attention."

Jeffrey leaned back in his chair, formed a pistol with his two index fingers, and rubbed the tip of his nose with it. I'd only been in his firm for two and a half months, but I'd learned the first week that pistol-fingers meant he felt he had the upper hand.

I will not squirm, I told myself firmly. *No more little outbursts. And no more information.*

"I have very little experience with arrangements of this kind," he said, lowering the pistol only enough to uncover his mouth. "And what I have had has not been positive."

He stopped, obviously waiting for me to defend myself. I didn't.

"If I knew more about what you were up against..." he said.

No way. Nothing doing, I thought. *You are not going to make me vulnerable.*

"Am I prying?" he said.

"I think you're well enough acquainted with my work to know I will get the job done and done well, no matter what schedule I keep." I looked at the file and then at him and waited for an answer. *If he said no,* I told myself, *then maybe I'd beg.*

He pistoled his nose a few more times and, still leaning back like the Godfather, said, "Two weeks."

"Excuse me?" The words *I'm giving you two weeks' notice* whipped through my head.

"We'll give this arrangement two weeks and then review it. If you come up short, I'll expect you back in the office full-time."

I stood up and thanked him coolly—giving him a you-really-didn't-have-any-other-choice smile—and left his office. Then I closed the oak door behind me and sagged against it. *What would I have done if he hadn't said yes?*

All My Tomorrows

by Al and JoAnna Lacy, The Orphan Train Trilogy, Book Two
ISBN 1-59052-130-7, U.S. Suggested Retail Price: $11.99
368 pages, trade paperback, Fiction/General/Historical
Reader's Group Discussion Questions Available

June 2003

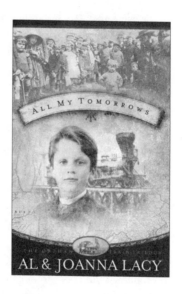

Sixty-two abandoned children leave New York on a train headed west, oblivious of what's in store. But their paths are being watched by someone who carefully plans all their tomorrows.

Al loves to read books on American history. That was how we learned about the Orphan Trains, a fascinating chapter of history that seems to have been overlooked in the textbooks. We found ourselves captivated by the true stories of hundreds of orphans—their tragedies, their fears, and their bare existence on New York City's streets—but also their joy when they found new homes in the West.

These stories are vastly different than anything else we have ever written. Seeing history through the eyes of children will deeply touch your heart and make these books impossible to set down. We also think you'll find this trilogy filled with our faith—gained from so many years of serving the Lord and trusting His written Word.

In *All My Tomorrows,* Johnny Smith's widower father is a New York City policeman who is killed in the line of duty. Johnny's dream had been to follow his father's footsteps and be a law officer. He is taken out West on an orphan train and indeed realizes his dream when he grows up.

When you've finished this book, we hope you'll not only have been entertained, but changed—inspired to walk closer to the Lord than ever before.

Al & JoAnna Lacy

SAMPLE CHAPTER

High in the Colorado Rockies, the sun was setting as outlaws Shad Gatlin and Bart Caddo halted their horses a few yards from the mouth of a cave. Gatlin and Caddo had traded off keeping their hostage in the saddle while they rode.

At the moment, Gatlin had Johnny Smith on his horse with him. Caddo dismounted. "I'll check the cave out, Shad." He pulled out his revolver and drew back the hammer. "Be right back."

Gatlin nodded. "We'll wait right here."

When his partner disappeared into the dark cave, Gatlin gazed around as the boy sat quietly in front of him. The shadows of the deep crags stretched from the west, and between them streamed a red-gold light. The sunset was a clear picture of sunshine losing its fire. Fleecy orange clouds rested over the lofty mountain peaks. A sailing eagle dotted the blue sky directly above them, its shrill cry echoing over the high country.

Johnny looked up at the majestic bird and wished he was free like the eagle. Seconds later, it sailed silently out of sight.

The silence around them was unbroken now, and a soft breeze, laden with the incense of pine, touched their faces.

Suddenly the silence was broken by a loud roar inside the cave, followed by three gunshots. A startled Johnny Smith jerked in the saddle, grabbing the pommel. Three more shots came from the cave while Shad Gatlin was swinging out of the saddle, pulling his gun. He headed toward the cave, calling over his shoulder, "You stay put, kid!"

Just as Gatlin reached the cave, Bart Caddo came out, gun in hand. Smoke was drifting upward from the muzzle. "I ran into a black female bear in there, Shad. She was way back at the end of the cave. She's dead now."

Gatlin shoved his gun back in its holster. "Well, let's drag her carcass outta there. I ain't wantin' to sleep in there with a dead bear."

"Me, neither. She ain't terribly big. Won't be hard for the two of us to get her outta there."

Gatlin turned and looked at Johnny. "Okay, kid, get down and come to the cave with us."

There was a fearful look on the boy's face as he slid from the saddle and walked toward the outlaws.

When they moved inside, Gatlin pointed to a spot just inside the cave's mouth. "Siddown right there, kid. And don't you move."

Instantly, Johnny dropped to the floor of the cave and sat with his back against the rugged rock wall. He watched as the two men moved back into the shadows and could barely see them as they grabbed the dead bear by the hind feet and dragged her toward the cave's mouth. Johnny focused on the black ball of fur as they dragged her past him, noting that her eyes were wide open in death. The outlaws dragged the bear outside and left the carcass under a tall spruce tree.

When they returned to the cave, Gatlin was carrying the rope he had used to bind Johnny up each night.

"Okay, kid, lie down right there so's I can tie you up. We've got to go out and find firewood so we can cook supper."

Johnny obeyed by stretching out on the dirt floor, intimidation showing in his eyes.

While Gatlin was cinching up the rope on his wrists and ankles, he said, "If you ever try to escape, kid, I promise I'll kill you for sure. Got that?"

"Yes, sir."

"Good. I'll untie you when we get back, so you can eat."

Twilight was settling over the mountains as the outlaws left the cave and vanished from Johnny's sight. Lying there, he thought of his father. He told himself if his father was a western lawman, he would come to his rescue. Justin Smith would find a way to get the drop on the bad men and free his son.

Tears filled the boy's eyes. His lips quivered. "But this can't happen because Dad lies in a cold, dark grave in the cemetery back in Manhattan." He sniffed and choked on his tears. "Oh, Dad, I miss you so much! I miss you too, Mom. Why did both of you have to die?"

Johnny's tears had dried up by the time he heard the outlaws coming toward the cave. It was now almost totally dark.

Gatlin and Caddo laid half of the broken tree limbs on the ground at the center of the cave's mouth, and laid the rest of it close by for future use. They pulled dried pine needles and cones from their pockets and set them close to the wood. Gatlin pulled out a match, struck it, and put the flame on the needles and cones. Flames flared up instantly, throwing light all around the cave.

Gatlin stood over Johnny and laughed. "Well whattya know! You're still here, eh, kid? I figured while we were gone that she-bear's mate would find her dead body over there under that tree and come in here ready to rip up whoever was in the cave."

Caddo chuckled. "Yeah, I figured all we'd find of you was your clean bones."

Johnny looked up at both men grimly.

The outlaws had stolen food, tin cups, coffee, coffeepot, and a skillet from a house they had burglarized in the small town of Florissant, just west of Pike's Peak. They went outside to the horses and took the goods from the saddlebags. While Johnny looked on from the floor of the cave, they started cooking supper.

Soon the sound of hot meat was crackling in the skillet while Shad Gatlin leaned over it, stirring the meat around. Bart Caddo was busy with the small coffeepot.

Johnny knew the time planned by Gatlin to kill him had to be drawing near. The fear within him was like a worm crawling through his brain. Gatlin had warned him not to beg for his life anymore, but the twelve-year-old boy could not hold back. He drew a shuddering breath. "Mr. Gatlin?"

Still stirring the crackling meat, Gatlin swung his gaze to Johnny. "Yeah?"

"Won't you please let me go? You and Mr. Caddo are safe now. If there were lawmen on your trail, they would have shown up by now. You don't need me as a hostage anymore."

Gatlin and Caddo exchanged glances by the firelight, then Gatlin grinned at the boy. "You're right, kid. We don't need you as a hostage anymore. Bart and I were talkin' about it when we were gatherin' the firewood. If that lame-brained Sheriff Clay Bostin was on our trail, he'd have been here before now."

Gatlin left the skillet on the fire and rose to his feet. Stepping to where Johnny lay, he looked down at him. "Bostin told me I was through killin'. Well, he was wrong."

Johnny's mouth went dry as Gatlin pulled his gun.

The outlaw chuckled dryly. "We need to get rid of you, all right, kid. You're eatin' food Bart and I need for ourselves. Not only that, but one of us has to have you in our saddle all the time we're ridin'."

Gatlin snapped the hammer back.

Johnny's eyes widened and the firelight cast a gray luminescence on his face.

Gatlin said icily, "I'll just kill you now, and get it over with."

Still holding the coffeepot, Bart Caddo was enjoying the terror he saw in Johnny's eyes as Gatlin aimed the muzzle at the boy's trembling head.

Suddenly a voice from the darkness outside barked, "Drop the gun, Gatlin, or you're dead!"

Both outlaws, as well as a terrified Johnny Smith, looked into the darkness toward the sound of the voice. The owner of the voice took a step into the vague light of the fire, which showed them Sheriff Clay Bostin standing just outside the cave with a cocked Colt .45 in each hand.

In a quick desperate move, Gatlin brought his gun up, swinging the muzzle toward the sheriff. Bostin's right-hand gun spit fire. Gatlin buckled, dropped his gun, and while he was falling, Bart Caddo dropped the coffeepot and whipped out his revolver.

Before he could bring it into play, Bostin's left-hand gun roared, and Caddo went down like a rock, never to move again.

Seeing that Gatlin was still breathing, Bostin kicked his gun deep into the darkness of the cave, then holstered both guns and knelt beside the boy. "Johnny, you all right?"

A relieved Johnny Smith found his voice. "Yes, sir, Sheriff. I'm all right. How'd you know my name?"

"The Children's Aid Society sponsors told me."

"Oh."

Bostin saw the relief displayed on the boy's face as he

began untying him. When the knots were loose, Bostin pulled the ropes away. "Can you get up?"

"Yes, sir." And with that, Johnny sprang to his feet, rubbing his wrists and running his gaze to Shad Gatlin.

Bostin took a step toward the outlaw and looked down at him.

Gatlin's face was a twisted mass of pain as he stared up at the sheriff with glassy eyes. He choked, then ejected a vile oath, cursing Bostin. "One…more second…and I would have…killed the…kid."

"I told you that you were through killing."

Gatlin swore at him again, and with that, he breathed out his last breath. His body went limp and his head fell to the side, his eyes frozen open.

Bostin leaned over and forced the eyelids shut. "Bad thing, Gatlin, going out into eternity cursing."

The sheriff turned and looked at the boy. "I'm sorry you had to witness two men being killed, Johnny."

Johnny looked up at the tall lawman and met his gaze. "It's better than what would have happened if you hadn't shown up exactly when you did, sir." At that instant, tears welled up in Johnny's eyes. "Thank you for staying on our trail and for saving my life."

Bostin moved to the boy and folded him in his arms. "I knew Gatlin would kill you once he thought he was safe, Johnny. I had to catch up to him before it was too late. I wanted you to have all your tomorrows."

Bostin's last words touched Johnny deeply. He eased back in the sheriff's arms, wiped tears from his cheeks, and looked up into Bostin's eyes. "All my tomorrows. I never heard it put like that before, Sheriff."

Bostin grinned. "You have a right to live out the life that God gave you. I'm just glad He let me get here in time so I could have a part in making sure it didn't end tonight."

Johnny swallowed hard. "Me too."

Releasing the boy from his arms, the sheriff went to the fire and removed the skillet from the flames. "Johnny, I'm going to remove these corpses from the cave, then you and I can eat supper."

Johnny watched while the sheriff carried the lifeless bodies of the outlaws out of the cave a few yards to the side, where he laid them down and covered them completely with rocks.

He returned, and the two of them sat down on the floor of the cave close to the fire to eat the supper that the outlaws had prepared. Before they began, Clay Bostin said, "Johnny, I always thank the Lord for the food before I eat. I also want to thank Him for letting me get here before those outlaws took your life."

Johnny let a thin smile curve his lips. "Yes, sir."

When Bostin closed his prayer, they began to eat. "Johnny, how did you become an orphan? Did both of your parents die at the same time?"

"No, sir."

Johnny told about his mother's death over a year ago, then explained how his policeman father was killed when he shot it out with two bank robbers. He made sure Bostin knew that the robbers were killed too.

Bostin spoke his condolences in the deaths of both Johnny's parents. "I can tell you carry a great deal of pride in what your father was."

"You're right, Sheriff. Since I was quite small, I wanted to be a policeman when I grew up, but...well, I had thoughts about being something else when Dad was killed in the line of duty." He paused and let another smile curve his lips. "But now that I have seen you in action, I just might become a lawman here in the West when I grow up."

"Johnny, that would be good. The West will be in need of good lawmen when you grow into adulthood even more than it is now, the way the population is increasing."

"That's something to think about, sir." Johnny paused, then said, "Sheriff Bostin, when we get back to Colorado Springs, I need to somehow make contact with the Children's Aid Society in New York so they will know I'm all right, and they can pick me up when the next orphan train comes through. I need to go on until some man and his wife choose me so they can be my foster parents and take me into their home."

"I'll have you back in Colorado Springs in three or four days. I'll help you make contact with the Society by wire."

"That'll really be swell, sir. I appreciate it very much."

"Glad to help."

When supper was over, Bostin added wood to the fire. "Johnny, I'll be right back. I have to go out and get my Bible out of the saddlebags. I always read my Bible before going to bed."

Johnny blinked. "Oh. All right."

The sheriff was back within a short time, and as he sat down beside Johnny, the boy looked at the Bible. "I've only seen the inside of a Bible a few times in my life."

Bostin smiled. "Well, you're welcome to read this one anytime you want. How about right now, though, we read it together?"

"I'd like that, sir. I've always wondered about a lot of things that people have told me are in the Bible."

"Oh, really?"

"Mm-hmm."

"What, for instance?"

"Well, when people die, they don't come back from the dead. But I've been told that in the Bible, God's prophets raised people from the dead, and so did Jesus Christ."

"That's right."

"And they say that Jesus even came back from the dead."

"He sure did."

"How could that be?"

"It was done by the power of God, Johnny. It is God who gives life in the first place. If He wants to give life back to someone who had died, He sure can do it."

Johnny pondered those words for a moment. "Well, that does make sense, sir. I hadn't thought about it like that. I guess God can do anything He wants, huh?"

"He sure can."

Johnny frowned. "Something else, Sheriff."

"Mmm-hmm?"

"I have a hard time believing there's a place called hell where people burn forever."

"God says there is." He opened the Bible. "Let me show you."

Bostin turned to Psalm 9. He angled the Bible toward the fire so Johnny could see it. "Read me verse 17."

Johnny focused on it. "'The wicked shall be turned into hell, and all the nations that forget God.' Who's the wicked, Sheriff?"

"People who never receive the Lord Jesus Christ as their Saviour."

"Oh."

Bostin flipped to Isaiah 14. "Johnny, do you know who Lucifer is?"

"No, sir."

"Do you know who Satan is?"

"The devil."

"Right. Well, when Satan was first created, God gave him the name Lucifer. Here in this passage, Lucifer has sinned against God. Look what God says to him in verse 15. Read it to me."

Johnny licked his lips. "'Yet thou shalt be brought down to hell, to the sides of the pit.'"

"Now keep that in mind," said Bostin, turning to the New Testament. "Look what Jesus said here in Matthew chapter 25, Johnny. Before I have you read it, let me explain that when Lucifer was cast out of heaven, there was a great number of angels who took his side and went with him."

"Really?"

"Really. In this passage, Jesus is talking about the day of the last judgment. He will have the saved people at His right hand, and the lost people at His left hand. He speaks of Himself in verse 41 and what He is going to say to those who are lost. Read it to me."

"'Then shall he say also unto them on the left hand, Depart from me, ye cursed, into everlasting fire, prepared for the devil and his angels.'"

"You see, Johnny, God didn't create hell for human beings, He created it for the devil and his angels. But when sinners refuse to come to God for salvation His way, He has nowhere else to put them. You see that lost human beings are going to the same hell. And what kind of fire did Jesus say it is?"

Johnny looked back at the verse. "Everlasting fire."

"Mm-hmm. Now look down at verse 46. Jesus says of the lost people, 'And these shall go away into everlasting punishment: but the righteous into life eternal.' What kind of punishment is it?"

"Everlasting, sir."

"What kind of fire is it, according to what Jesus said in verse 41?"

"Everlasting."

"That means both the fire and the punishment will go on forever, doesn't it?"

"Yes, sir."

"There are many other passages of Scripture that tell of the burning hell where people go when they die if they die without Jesus Christ as their Saviour, Johnny, but I think for the moment, this is enough for you to see that there is a burning place called hell that actually exists."

Johnny nodded. "Yes, sir. I believe it."

"Good. The next few days as we travel, I'll show you more on the subject. We'll also look at passages that discuss the wrath of God against sin. Right now, I want to show you some other things."

Before they began to read more, Bostin could see that the Scriptures Johnny had already seen had stamped a deep impression on him. He then took the boy to passages that deal with salvation and what Jesus did on the cross for sinners in His death, burial, and resurrection, and had him read them aloud to him.

Since this was all new to Johnny, Bostin stopped there and told him they would read more tomorrow night. He told Johnny they would have prayer, and while he was praying, the sheriff asked God to help Johnny to understand the gospel that he might be saved. He also prayed that the Lord would place Johnny in the home where He wanted him.

Both those requests touched Johnny's heart.

During the next two days, Clay and Johnny talked much about salvation while Johnny rode the horse Shad Gatlin had stolen. The other stolen horse followed as led by the sheriff from his saddle.

On both nights, the two read Scriptures on the subject of God's wrath against sin, salvation, heaven, and hell. The sheriff discussed them with the boy.

At the end of the third day, they were within less than three hours' ride from Colorado Springs when they stopped and made camp for the night. By this time, the Holy Spirit had done His work in Johnny's heart, and when it was Bible reading time beside the campfire, Johnny told the sheriff he wanted to be saved. Clay Bostin had the joy of leading the boy to Jesus.

After Johnny had gone to sleep in Shad Gatlin's bedroll, Sheriff Clay Bostin lay awake in his own bedroll, praising the Lord for Johnny's salvation.

As the campfire dwindled, the shadows of the pines closed in darker and darker upon the circle of fading light. A cool wind fanned the embers, whipped up flakes of white ashes, and moaned through the trees. Clay looked up and marveled at the beauty of God's handiwork above him. The sky was a massive black dome spangled with twinkling white stars.

While studying the dazzling heavens, Clay thought about the strange stirring that had been going on in his heart since before he and Johnny had started their trip back to Colorado Springs. The stirring had only grown stronger since then.

He pondered the fact that he and Mary had been married for over four years, and that they learned only recently that she would never be able to bear children. He thought about their attempts at finding a child on the orphan trains, but how the Lord gave them no direction on choosing any of the children.

Clay thought about last Wednesday, and how they had planned again to prayerfully look the children over at the depot, but Johnny Smith was abducted by Shad Gatlin, and Clay had to ride away in pursuit immediately. He and Mary were not able to talk about her looking the children over by herself. He wondered if she had chosen a child.

He thought about the genuine affinity he had felt toward Johnny—coupled with the strange stirring in his heart—even before they began the return trip. Lying there beneath the stars, he looked toward heaven and said in a low whisper, "Lord, I know You have put it in my heart that even if Mary chose another child at the depot last Wednesday, we are also to take Johnny into our home as his foster parents. You have made it so clear. I will talk to him about it in the morning."

After thanking the Lord from the depths of his heart for letting him save Johnny's life and for allowing him to lead the boy to Jesus, Clay fell asleep thinking about the moment he would talk to the boy in the morning about living in the Bostin home as their foster son.

A Steadfast Surrender

by Nancy Moser
ISBN 1-59052-143-9, U.S. Suggested Retail Price: $11.99
350 pages, trade paperback, Fiction/General/Contemporary
Reader's Group Discussion Questions Available

June 2003

Claire Adams has wealth, power, and potential. She needs nothing and thinks she has everything...until God offers her the chance of a lifetime in Steadfast, Kansas.

My objective for writing *A Steadfast Surrender* was to get readers to completely surrender to God. Most believers have surrendered to some extent—accepting Christ as Savior is a huge point of surrender. Yet there is so much more. It's like our life is a big dresser drawer. We open up some of the drawers and show the contents willingly. But there are other drawers we'd rather keep closed. Locked. And yet in the Christian life—if there is growth going on—God will give us the opportunity to open up each and every drawer, to take out the contents before His eyes and display them, waiting for His comments and suggestions. His forgiveness. The question is: Will we? Whether our drawers are full of money, career issues, pride, love, sex, family, control…we can't hold anything back from Him. We can't fling our bodies against the dresser, saying, "No! Don't look in there!"

We need to get to the point of opening the drawers willingly, offering Him a blanket "Yes!" even before He's asked a question. We need to wake up in the morning saying yes to Him. Yes, to whatever He wills. There is no greater joy or point of excitement than in a steadfast surrender.

Nancy Moser

SAMPLE CHAPTER

The intercom buzzed. "Call on line one, Claire. It's your pastor."

Claire could hardly skip that call—and didn't want to. The previous Sunday they had dedicated the mosaic altar she'd created and donated. He was probably calling to share some compliments with her.

She picked up the phone. "Pastor Joe. All's well with the altar, I hope?"

"An altar fit for a King. We're extremely grateful for it."

"You're welcome."

"But I have a favor to ask you."

"Uh-oh. I feel a request for a matching baptismal font coming on."

"Actually, I need your culinary expertise."

For a moment she was speechless. "Surely you jest."

"Oh, you'll do fine. We have the administrator of a Denver shelter visiting. She's been talking at the circle meetings and will give a speech at the congregational dinner tomorrow night. She's staying at the Martin's. But tomorrow the Martin's have some softball function for the kids, and Molly and I have a bowling tournament—"

"How's your game?"

"I've hit three digits."

"Ooh. Strike three, you're out."

"Wrong kind of strike, Claire. Anyway, we wondered if you would entertain the administrator tomorrow noon. Have her over for lunch."

During the divorce, Claire took solace in the church she previously ignored and discovered the benefits of becoming a joiner. She was now on Pastor Joe's ready-willing-and-able list of volunteers and didn't really mind. Giving back eased the pain of what she'd given up.

"You'd like her, Claire."

She sighed. "Does she have a name?"

"Michelle Jofsky."

"Wouldn't you rather have a couple do this?"

"I think she's been coupled out. An afternoon woman-to-woman would probably be a relief. She's a baseball fan, just like you. Sometimes eating pizza and watching baseball is a thousand times more satisfying than a four-course meal."

That made it easier. "Pizza I can handle. Baseball, huh? A Royals fan, I hope?"

"Cubs. You'll have to duke it out."

"I'll kick in my Christian tolerance. For one afternoon. As a favor to you."

"And God."

"Who we both wish was a more avid Royals fan."

"I'll call Michelle and tell her to be over at noon. And Claire? This is a good thing you're doing, and I'm proud of you. But…"

"But what?"

"Be good. Okay?"

"Hey, you started it. But never fear. I'll give it my best shot."

Michelle Jofsky tried to block out the noise of the Martin boys arguing over a video game in the next room. She tried to concentrate on the Bible in her lap. It wasn't easy.

She enjoyed traveling and talking to churches about the Salvation Shelter where she worked. And she really didn't mind staying in people's homes. Most of the time. It wasn't that she was used to silence. She wasn't. Her apartment was above the shelter and there was always noise. People noise. Since being at the Martins' she'd realized it was mechanical noise that grated her nerves: TV, computer, stereo. How could these people ever hope to hear God if they never allowed silence into their lives? She'd said something to the youngest boy, but he merely turned the volume down from deafening to annoying.

She'd escaped to her room, starting her so-called quiet time with a prayer for tolerance and a dose of God-sent concentration. She opened her Bible at random, willing God to lead her time with Him. It opened to Colossians. She read: "Devote yourselves to prayer, being watchful and thankful. And pray for us, too, that God may open a door for our message, so that we may proclaim the mystery of Christ, for which I am in chains. Pray that I may proclaim it clearly, as I should. Be wise in the way you act toward outsiders; make the most of every opportunity. Let your conversation be always full of grace, seasoned with salt, so that you may know how to answer everyone."

She looked up. Interesting. Especially considering all the speaking she'd done in the last two days. And tomorrow night was the big congregational dinner. Good words. Appropriate—

A tap on the door. "Michelle? Phone."

She left the guest room to take the phone in the kitchen. It was Pastor Joe.

"How you faring, Michelle?"

She glanced at the alien battle being played out on the computer screen across the room and remembered the verse's admonition to have her conversation "full of grace." "I'm doing fine, Joe. What's up?"

"How'd you like to watch baseball and eat pizza with Claire Adams, one of our single parishioners?"

Baseball, pizza, single… "That sounds heavenly."

He chuckled. "I thought you'd say that. And I think you'll find Claire a fascinating woman. She's a mosaic artist on the verge of famous. She's had shows in London, Venice, Cincinnati…"

"Cincinnati?"

"I guess art appreciation knows no bounds. Noon tomorrow, okay? Claire's looking forward to the opportunity to meet you, one-on-one."

The verse offered a reprise: *Make the most of every opportunity.* Michelle's insides pulled, and she caught her breath. She knew what that feeling meant. This was not going to be an ordinary pizza lunch. "I look forward to it."

She loved when God got her guessing.

By the time Claire got off the phone with Pastor Joe, she was on the verge of late. In order to get to her meeting at the gallery on time, she took a short cut and got lost. Now, though she'd figured out where she was, she had no choice but to grab some fast food. Fast.

She stopped at a traffic light and scoped out the neighborhood. Garbage hugged the curb, there were bars on the windows of a beauty shop, and an abandoned car was permanently installed on a side street with a cat lounging on its hood. It was not the best part of town, but it would have to do.

Claire spotted a McDonald's one block ahead and turned into the parking lot, heading toward the drive-through. It was blocked with orange traffic cones and a sign: *Please excuse the inconvenience. Come inside to order.*

Come inside? Who had time to go inside?

Her stomach rumbled its vote. She'd have to make the time.

Claire parked her silver Lexus close to the front door where she could keep tabs on it. She went inside and was relieved the line was short. She ordered a #1, super-sized, with a Coke. She handed the teenager a fifty. The boy studied it as if it were foreign currency.

"Got anything smaller? We're not supposed to take bigger than a twenty."

Claire opened her billfold and fanned through the bills. She'd just cashed the check she'd received for the sale of her latest commission—a mosaic coffee table—and had specifically asked for hundreds, not wanting her billfold to be too thick. "Sorry, that's the smallest I have."

She suddenly noticed she had an audience. Seven sets of eyes bounced from her billfold to her face, then back again. Her cheeks grew hot. Her heart skipped a beat. She folded the billfold shut.

A manager walked near the boy. "Go ahead, Marlon. Give the lady her change."

Marlon handed Claire her change and her order.

Claire hurried to her car, got in, and locked the doors. She put the sack on the seat so she could tuck the change away. But when she opened her billfold, she lingered, seeing with fresh eyes what the people in the restaurant had seen.

The stack of twenty-five hundreds stared back at her. The crispness of the bills contrasted with the wrinkled, much-used bills she'd gotten for change. Two-thousand-five-hundred dollars. Claire's average weekly amount. Cash for spending money.

Most people would have accepted that amount as a decent *month's* wages.

She'd just paid for a fast food lunch with a fifty-dollar bill. *"Sorry, that's the smallest I have."* She hadn't meant to sound uppity, but the very fact that she thought nothing of paying with fifties and hundreds was as symptomatic as it was ridiculous. Was she so immune to wealth that she could flaunt it with abandon? Did she care nothing about the reactions of those around her, who by seeing her riches might feel their own lack more deeply? To say nothing of the temptation.

She looked at the inside of her car. It still had the new car smell and the IN-TRANSIT sticker on the back window. A CD-player, cell phone, cassette. Air-conditioning, anti-lock brakes, cruise control, dual air-bags. A laptop computer sat on the floor of the passenger side, safely tucked away in a leather case.

Even her clothes...no funky Bohemian attire for this artist. For some reason people expected her to wear Indian-print skirts, sandals, and have long hair that had more *poof* than style. Claire would never tolerate being a stereotype.

When she was in her studio—dirty with tile dust, metal shavings, and grout—she opted for comfort rather than style. But in public she leaned toward Armani or her suit of the day, which happened to sport a Donna Karan label. To obtain the impeccable look of success, she only bought the best. Her shoes and matching purse had been purchased from a pricey catalog, and a Rolex adorned her wrist. One of two she owned. One gold. One silver. To match her accessories of the day.

Her stomach clenched. She fumbled with the keys. When the engine revved to life an old man near the entrance of the restaurant looked up, then away, as he shuffled to a trashcan, pushed open the swinging lid, and grabbed a crushed sack.

What's he doing?

Claire sat transfixed. The man opened the sack and peered inside. His hand disappeared, coming out with two French fries, which he stuffed into his mouth. Another dig brought out the last few bites of a hamburger. He shoved it in his mouth, licking his fingers.

Claire smelled her own lunch, sitting unopened on the seat beside her. Super-sized. The sheer quantity of the meal repulsed her.

Before the thought moved from synapse to synapse, Claire grabbed the sack and the drink, opened the car door, and walked to the man. "Sir?"

He looked up. There was a crumb poised on his whiskers.

She held the food in his direction. "I've already eaten. Would you like this meal? It's a Big Mac. Large fries." She tried a smile.

The man looked at the sack, practically drooling. Then he squinted at Claire and smiled back. "That depends. What's the drink?"

"Coke."

The man nodded. "Nifty. You got a deal."

Claire returned the nod and headed back to her car, feeling virtuous. She noticed her billfold on the seat. An idea overwhelmed her.

No, you're thinking crazy...a meal is one thing, but—

She turned back to the man. He was walking away. "Sir?"

He turned.

Claire looked down at her shoes. How could she do this without hurting his pride? "You...do you have a wife?"

"Not anymore."

Oh dear. "You have kids?"

"Two or three."

Whew. Claire reached into the car and grabbed the bill-fold. She withdrew the bills, not even looking at them, afraid she would chicken out. "Here. Buy them a Christmas present."

The man stared at the wad of hundreds. He squinted at the summer sun. "But it's June."

"Birthday then. Buy them something special." She backed toward the car.

The man stared at the money, then at her. "Why you doing this?"

Claire bumped into the car door. She reached backward for the handle, then shrugged and managed a shaky laugh. "I have no idea."

The man scratched his head. "Whatever the reason, God bless you, ma'am."

Claire's heart beat through her blouse. She felt something swell inside her like a dam ready to burst. She got in the car and put it in reverse, nearly backing into a passing vehicle. As she pulled around the building, she noticed two cars using the drive-through.

There were no orange cones in sight.

Claire found a day-old donut on the studio table that served as layout space, lunch table, and chair if she felt the need to gaze at her work from a new angle. She poured a cup of coffee and sat down to eat. Her heels skimmed the concrete floor.

From across the warehouse-sized space, her head metal-worker, Darla, turned off her blowtorch, flipped up her mask, and came toward her. "Those are from yesterday, you know."

She shrugged.

Darla tilted her head. "You look…odd. Didn't it go well at

the gallery?"

"I never got to the gallery."

"Why not?"

She thought about telling Darla about giving all her money to the old man, but stopped. Not only would her friend think she was insane, she had the feeling if she shared her good deed with anyone, it would be spoiled. But oh, how she would like to brag. She took another bite of donut. "Long story for another day, another time. How are things going here?"

Darla studied her a moment longer before pointing to where she'd been working. "The base for the Oswald dining-room table should be ready this afternoon, and Sandy is putting away the shipment of smalti that came in this morning. Everything should be ready to go. All you need to do is finish up the mosaic."

She snickered. "Inspiration on demand, huh?"

"You always manage to come through."

Claire swung her legs back and forth. "I don't feel very creative right now."

Darla changed her weight to the other foot. "What's wrong? You seem restless."

What's wrong? What's right? What's real? What's unreal?

When Claire didn't answer, Darla continued. "They're expecting it the end of this week. Do you want Lana to call and tell them it will be late?"

Claire took a deep breath, then removed her jacket and headed to where her work clothes were kept. "No. I'll get to it. Right now."

Darla followed her. "Claire…what aren't you telling me?"

She forced a smile as she hung up her jacket. "It's nothing for you to worry about. Honestly. It's nothing for anyone to worry about. It's a good thing. I think."

"A good thing. Even more reason to share."

Claire pinched her lower lip. "But not now. Not yet." She took a cleansing breath. "Now go on. There's work to do."

And thinking.

Saturday noon, the doorbell rang. Claire answered it to find a fiftyish woman holding a pizza box while the pizza delivery car drove away. It took Claire a moment to sort through the scene. "Michelle?"

The woman raised the box and inhaled. "I smell pepperoni."

"Good nose." Claire took the pizza and stood aside so her guest could enter. Claire dug into her jeans pocket for the money she'd put there for the pizza man. "Here, you beat me to it."

Michelle waved the money away. "I'll supply the pizza if you supply an unlimited supply of iced tea."

Claire smiled. She liked her. "One cold one coming up."

They moved into the kitchen area. Claire got out plates and napkins. The smell of pepperoni and cheese filled the air. She noted Michelle was a good six inches shorter than she was and fifty pounds heavier. But what Michelle lacked in height, she made up for in pluck. Claire liked how she made herself right at home, opening the cupboards, getting out two glasses, and filling them with ice.

"Nice place."

"Thanks." Since Claire gave Ron the house, she'd moved into this three-bedroom townhouse. Although it was a step down in size, it was comparable in quality and luxury. Not that she *needed* marble countertops or crown moldings, but she was used to them. "The game doesn't start for a half hour."

Michelle pulled out a stool at the breakfast bar. "Then let's sit here."

"Sure." As Claire sat and they started eating, she suddenly realized she needed to come up with conversation. She'd been counting on the game negating any need for her to be wise and witty.

Michelle beat her to it. "Pastor Joe says you're rich and famous."

Claire choked. Michelle patted her on the back.

"You okay?"

Claire took a sip of tea and wiped her mouth with a paper napkin. "You just surprised me, that's all. And Pastor Joe told *me* to be good?"

Michelle shrugged and the glint in her eye hinted there was more to come. "I work in a facts-based business. I prefer to slog through bushes rather than beat around them."

"What bush are we talking about?"

"Money."

Claire's stomach sank. Pastor Joe was going to pay for making her spend the afternoon with a fund-raiser. If he'd wanted a donation he should have asked. She might as well get it over with, give the lady a check, and hope the baseball game would start early.

She stood to get her checkbook. "I can give you something for your shelter."

Michelle shook her head. She nipped a string of cheese with her fingers, then licked them noisily. "I don't want your money."

"But you said—"

"I said I wanted to *talk* about money, I didn't ask for any."

Claire returned to the stool. "You don't want my money?"

"Not your guilt money."

"Excuse me?"

Michelle shook her head while patting a napkin to her mouth as she finished chewing. "Maybe I'd better start over."

Claire took a sip of tea and set her glass down hard. "Maybe you'd better."

"I run a shelter for indigents in Denver."

"I know that."

"I live in a room on the second floor. I eat with the homeless. I have few possessions I call my own." She swiveled in her seat and extended an arm, taking in the hearth room, the breakfast area, and the kitchen. "You have so much."

This sounded like a trap. "But you don't want my money."

She held up a finger. "Your guilt money."

The appeal of Michelle Jofsky's make-herself-at-home nature dimmed. "If this is how you fund-raise, you'd better think of a new approach."

Michelle faced her, stool to stool. "That's just it. I don't think I'm here to get money from you."

"You don't *think*...?"

She took a breath. "I'm sorry. I'm being way too blunt. I get that way when I'm excited."

"And what are you excited about?"

"Opportunities."

"Such as?"

Michelle turned back to her pizza. "Are you open to Him, to *things?*"

Him. God. "What kind of things?"

Michelle looked at Claire straight on. "Feelings. Hunches."

"Women's intuition? That sort of thing?"

"Beyond that." She wiped her palms on her thighs. "Oh

dear, there's no subtle way to breach this thought I have, this notion, this nudge."

"Then just say it. I can take it. I promise."

Michelle studied her a moment. "I think you're the reason I came to Kansas City."

Claire finished chewing. She didn't like the sound of this. *Twilight Zone* was cancelled years ago. She did not need to experience one of the lost episodes. She got up from her stool. "Want some more tea?"

"No thanks."

Claire didn't either, but poured some anyway. She also took another slice of pizza, though the thought of eating more was unsettling.

"You want to know why I think you're the reason I came here?"

"I'm not sure. But tell me anyway." Claire mentally braced herself.

"The answer is: I don't know."

Claire's shoulders dropped. "Should I be relieved or disappointed?"

"I wish I could be more specific. Sometimes it is and sometimes it isn't. Specific, I mean."

"It?"

"My hunches. Feelings."

"This happens often?"

"Often enough."

"But you said you were a facts person. Hunches are not based on facts."

"Sure they are. It's a fact I got a feeling about you. I can choose to ignore it or accept it. Go with it. This time I went with it. I came here this afternoon, didn't I?"

"To tell me…?"

"I don't know."

Claire shook her head and glanced at the TV. *Come on game. Start!* "Are your hunches always so vague?"

"Not vague, just non-specific."

"I don't see the distinction."

"The urgings I have, the nudgings, are very real and more than mental. They're so strong they almost give me a physical push. I *know* I'm supposed to do something, I just don't know the details."

"Give me an example."

Michelle ran a finger across the condensation on her glass. Then she nodded. "Ten years ago, before I started to work at the shelter, I was walking in an industrial part of town when I had an urging to turn right and go down a specific street. I had no reason to turn, and to tell you the truth, I was running late and really needed to keep going. Since then I've learned it's best to follow through with these promptings. It's become an obligation."

"Who says?"

Michelle smiled. "We'll get to that. Anyway, I turned right. I hadn't been down that street before, but I knew it led to the railroad tracks. Yet there was a kind of purpose in my walking, as if there was something I was supposed to see. So I kept my eye out for a reason I was being brought there; searching for the last piece to the puzzle. When I got to the tracks I saw a bunch of lean-tos, the kind the homeless make out of boxes and boards. More than anything, I wanted to turn around and get out of there. That kind of poverty and desperation made me uncomfortable, you know?"

"I can imagine."

"But then I saw an old man lying right next to the tracks, so close that his back was against a rail. Passed out. As soon as I saw him I felt a rumbling in my feet. The light of a train came closer. It blared its horn. It was like a scene in a movie. At first all I could do was shake my head no. This was *not* happening. Then I snapped out of it, ran to the man, and rolled him away from the tracks. Just in time. I saved him. Me following the nudge saved him."

"Very admirable. So you're here to save me, even if I'm *not* passed out in the path of an oncoming train?"

"But maybe you are."

Claire stood and paced near the counters. "Look around. I'm perfectly safe. No trains in sight."

"But you may be on the wrong track."

She'd had enough. "Excuse me, Ms. Jofsky. You don't know me well enough to know what track I'm on, much less if it's wrong, and I resent—"

Michelle pushed her plate away and rested her arms on the counter. She looked down at her clasped hands.

Her calm was infuriating. "Don't just sit there. Defend yourself." Michelle shook her head. The noncombative action took the steam out of Claire's engine. "You've got to admit it's mighty strange, you coming into my home, telling me you don't want my guilt-money, telling me you were sent here, telling me I'm on the wrong track and in the path of an oncoming train."

When Michelle looked up Claire started at the tenderness in the woman's eyes. "Let me back up to something I know for certain."

"Good idea."

"I believe we've each been created with a unique purpose.

We've been placed in this unique time, in this unique position and place, in this unique set of circumstances to *do* something unique. We just have to find out what it is. *You* need to find out what it is."

"And that's why you're here."

"Maybe." She took a deep breath and glanced at the front door. "When I drove up to this house I had a feeling…and when I came in and saw how you live and felt the wealth—"

"This place is hardly ostentatious. My ex is the showy one. This place is minimal compared to—"

Michelle raised a hand. "I'm not condemning you. Not at all. Earning a lot of money is not a sin. In the Bible, there were lots of rich people. King David and King Solomon were very rich, and God didn't hold their wealth against them." Her eyes lit up. She put a hand to her mouth. "Do you have a Bible?"

"Of course I have a Bible."

"Get it."

Claire retrieved it off her bedside table and held it out to Michelle, but Michelle didn't take it, pushing it back toward Claire. "No. It's for you to read. You to find."

"Find?"

"The verses that will help you understand."

"What verses are they?"

Michelle headed toward the door, her face drawn with a puzzled concentration. She stopped to answer. "Maybe the book of Mark…no. I won't say more. Read *the* Book, Claire. See where *He* takes you."

She opened the door.

"But the baseball—"

Michelle shook her head. "Some other time. Prayers to you, Claire. I think you may need them."

Sold Out

by Melody Carlson
Diary of a Teenage Girl series: Chloe, Book 2
ISBN 1-59052-141-2, U.S. Suggested Retail Price: $12.99
300 pages, trade paperback
Youth Children/Youth Interest/Teen Fiction
Reader's Group Discussion Questions Available

June 2003

Chloe Miller and her fellow band members must sort out their lives as they become a hit in the local community. Accustomed only to being scorned and marginalized, Chloe suddenly has to decide who her real friends are, and who's just along for the ride.

Now her generosity gets her in more trouble than ever. And all too soon after a talent scout from Nashville discovers the trio, their explosive musical ministry begins to encounter conflicts with family and school. Exhilarated yet frustrated, Chloe puts her dream in God's hands and prays for Him to work out the details.

❧

Chloe initially appears in Caitlin's Diary #3 *(Who I Am)* when Caitlin befriends Josh Miller's younger sister, a middle-school rebel. Chloe has offbeat clothes, spiked hair, and numerous piercings. Intelligent and musically gifted, Chloe's biggest question is about God. But after she meets him head-on, in a deserted graveyard, her life is never the same.

Readers have loved following Caitlin's spiritual journey, but Chloe offers them a slightly edgier ride. Chloe—not your typical teen—will offer her intelligence, insight, and giftedness as she lives her life and interacts with other non-mainstream teens, trying to reach them for God. She will learn some tough lessons about following God, her heart, and her dreams as she develops as a young musician and performer.

Melody Carlson

Sample Chapter

Friday, April 11

Six months ago (to this very day!) I gave my life to God. And right now I feel like a complete failure. I can just see God shaking His head at me, thinking: "Get it together, girl!" Or maybe not—God is more mature than that, more gracious, more kind.

Yet who would've guessed that a day that started so well would go so crooked? Just goes to show you we don't have as much control over things as we'd like to believe. And even when we think we're doing everything right, it can still go wrong. Anyway, I got up early, spent some time with God, printed out copies of my latest song (for Allie and Laura to look over), and even rode my bike to school—part of my new "get fit" regime. I was feeling pretty good.

But now it seems I can't even do the simplest of things! I mean, how many times have I read Jesus' words—where He tells us to love, not just our friends, but everyone, even our enemies? <u>How many times?</u> And, okay, I'll admit I still have a hard time loving my enemies. Take Tiffany Knight for instance. She's a pretty tough chick to love. Still, I ask for God's help on a regular basis, and I haven't done anything too lame lately. At least not to Tiffany.

Unfortunately I blew it with one of my very best friends today, and I can't really blame her for being mad at me right now. Actually, I'm still pretty ticked at her too, but I know I reacted wrongly, selfishly, stupidly even. Worst of all I feel like crud to have been so incredibly immature in front of a bunch of our friends. How moronic is that? I'm not blind. I know that people watch Allie, Laura, and me to see how we act, how we treat others.

Ever since our band, Redemption, has been getting better known, it's as if we've suddenly turned into God's poster kids—like no mistake will go unnoticed. It probably sounds as if I'm becoming a bit paranoid, but I don't think so. I think they ARE watching, and waiting…for days just like today. And really, I'm not complaining about that so much, because it's what I wanted. I do want my friends to see my life for what it is—up close and personal—but hopefully so they can see God in me. Not me acting like a total jerk. That's why I'm infuriated at myself right now. I feel as though I made God look bad, and I hate when that happens.

It all started out in the cafeteria. Laura and Allie and I were eating together like we often do, although not always. Laura's friends LaDonna and Mercedes were sitting with us too, along with a few others, and we were all having a pretty good time until Laura pulled out a copy of my latest song, the one I'd given her just this morning. I'd hoped we could pull it together to perform next month at the All God's Children festival. And this is especially important to me because the money we make there will go to such a great cause.

But anyway, it became quite obvious that Laura didn't like my song. And now that I think about it, she seemed to be in a fairly obnoxious mood today. She'd already yipped at LaDonna about something or other and had been complaining about lunch (although that's understandable).

"This stanza is so cliché." Her voice seemed to take on that somewhat superior tone that she uses occasionally. But then I sort of understand how she's like that sometimes. I think it's her way of saying, "Hey, I'm important too."

"Cliché?" I leaned over to see which line she was referring to, at the same time telling myself to just chill, don't take offense. I mean, Laura has every right to her opinion.

"Yeah, it's just kind of boring."

"Boring?" Now that seemed a rather strong opinion to me.

"Aw, it's not that bad," injected Allie before taking a bite of pizza.

Laura pressed her lips together. "Well, maybe boring is the wrong word. But I guess the words fall kind of flat on me."

"Flat?" I'm sure my voice sounded a little flat at this point. I was starting to think it might've been nice if Laura had saved her criticism until later—a more private time when not so many ears were tuned in. I suppose this means I still have a problem with my pride. I glanced around the group and pretended not to care what they or anyone else thought, but I could see they were pretty amused by our little conflict. I shrugged. "Well, if you really don't like it—"

"It's not that I don't like the <u>whole</u> song. But this verse right here feels so cliché."

"Yeah, you mentioned that." It's possible I snapped those words out.

"You don't have to get so offended, Chloe."

"I'm not." I folded my arms across my chest and desperately tried to act nonchalant. "But you don't have to be so critical, either."

"Sorry." I could hear the irritation intensifying her voice. "I didn't know you had such thin skin."

"Well, think about it, Laura. No writer likes being told she's '*cliché.*'"

"Fine. I guess I should've just told you that I'm sure I've heard this line in about a dozen other songs."

"<u>What</u> songs?" I realized my voice was increasing in volume now, but it seemed as if she was taking this whole thing way too far.

"Oh, lots of songs. I think it might've even been in an old Beatles song—"

"So you're saying the Beatles are cliché?"

She rolled her eyes at me. "No, I think <u>you</u> are cliché."

"Well, thanks a lot!" I snatched the paper from her hands and stood.

"Don't get mad, Chloe." This came from Allie. And no defense of my lyrics either; she seemed to assume this was just <u>my</u> problem.

"I'm *not* mad." I picked up my tray. "I think I need a change of scenery is all." And then I walked over to where Allie and I used to always eat, but now only eat sometimes. Today Jake, Cesar, Spencer, and a new girl named Marissa were sitting there.

"Hey, Chloe," called Cesar. "I thought maybe you'd ditched us for good."

I set down my tray. "Nah. It's just that we've been using lunchtime to work on some things for the next concert." Okay, that was partially true, but not completely. And I guess they saw through me.

Especially Jake. He looked unconvinced. "Aw, don't give us that bull, Chloe. We all know that Laura thinks she's too good for us. I used to think she was kinda cool, but now I think she's just like the rest of them." He glanced back to the table I'd just abandoned. "Even now she's looking over here like we're some nasty, trashy influence on you." He made a face imitating her.

I had to laugh. "No, that's not it. The reason she's scowling like that is because we just had a little snit."

"What about?" asked Marissa with obvious curiosity. "I thought you Christian kids always got along with each other."

Now I wished I'd kept my mouth shut. "Oh, it was nothing. She just didn't like a song I'd written."

Spencer laughed. "Oh yeah, I get it. Can't take the criticism, can you? Sure, it's fun when everyone's clapping and thinking you're great—"

"Man, are you in the wrong biz if you can't take the heat," added Cesar. "You ever read music reviews? Those critics can be pretty cruel, you know."

"I know and I would expect that kind of crud from a music critic. But it seems like your own band should be a little more understanding and supportive."

Marissa patted my shoulder in what seemed a somewhat demeaning way. "You're absolutely right, Chloe. And if I was in your band, I'd *never* pick on you."

I rolled my eyes. "Thanks, I feel so much better now."

"Yeah, too bad Marissa can't carry a tune," added Cesar. "You could throw Laura out and sign her up."

"Thanks, Julius." Marissa tossed him a look. She liked to call him 'Julius' to aggravate him—like for Julius Caesar (pronounced see-sir, when Cesar's name is actually pronounced say-zar).

Anyway, hoping to change the subject, I turned my attention to Marissa. "So, are you feeling better about your move now?" I asked. The last time she and I had spoken, she was still feeling depressed about changing schools in the middle of the year.

"I guess." She glanced around the table and smiled half-heartedly. "These guys are treating me pretty good."

Spencer stood. "Yeah, but she still won't go out with any of us." He nodded to Jake. "Wanna get some fresh air?"

I shook my head. "Man, you really need a new line, Spencer. That one's getting pretty frazzled, you know."

"Yeah," Marissa chimed in with a twinkle in her eye. "Why don't you just admit that you're going out behind the school to puff on some weed?"

Spencer glared at her then let loose with some profanity before he scuffled away, trying I'm sure to act cool. I have to admit that his language bothers me more than it used to, but I also remind myself that it's just where he's at right now. And I believe Jesus wants me to accept him—as he is.

I turned my attention back to Marissa. Now I need to point out that she's a really interesting looking girl—quite pretty actually, although I suspect she doesn't have a clue. She has this gorgeous long dark hair and startling green eyes that she outlines too heavily in black. Today she had on a short denim skirt and tall boots. "So how come you won't go out with any of these guys?" I asked.

She quickly at Cesar. "Just not with the ones who've asked."

So then I realized, with a slight jolt, that she's after him. But what's that to me? I'd already made it perfectly clear I wasn't interested in getting involved with Cesar right now anyway. Yet I did experience a teeny twinge of jealousy just then. Naturally I tried to conceal this with another question. "So what do you do for fun then?"

She shrugged. "Not much."

"You want to do something with Allie and me this weekend?"

Her eyes lit up. "Sure."

"Let me see what's up with Allie and then give you a call."

"Cool."

The bell started to ring and I picked up my tray. "Later," I said as I headed out. At the tray drop-off I saw Laura, and she had on a scowl that looked to be carved right into her forehead. "You didn't have to get into a huff like that, Chloe, just because you didn't like my opinion."

I shrugged as I dumped my tray. I suppose I still felt hurt, or maybe just sorry for myself. I know I wanted her to apologize to me first. And I'm sure if she'd shown the slightest degree of sympathy, the whole thing would've blown over right then and there. And I'd have apologized to her too. For sure. So why didn't we just resolve the whole stupid thing right then and there? Why go to the trouble to bear grudges when it only makes you feel horrible?

She nodded over to where Marissa and Cesar were just leaving the table. "Chloe, do you really think you should be hanging with those guys?"

"Those guys?" Okay, maybe I was just mad, but something about her tone ignited something in me. I suppose it was indignation. And I narrowed my eyes at her. "What exactly do you mean by that?"

"I just happen to think it's wrong, is all."

Well, this is when I lost it. I mean, it's not the first time Laura has pulled this, and today it just got to me. "What is it with you, Laura?" I asked loudly (stupidly drawing even more attention). "Why are you so down on absolutely everyone and everything? What kind of Christian are you supposed to be anyway?"

Her eyes flashed at me, but she said nothing, just turned away.

"Fine!" I shouted after her. "Be that way!"

"Time to lighten up," said Allie quietly, coming up from

behind and placing her hand on my shoulder. "Chill."

"Why?" I demanded. "Why do I need to chill when Laura goes around acting like she's God's special appointee to judge everyone?"

"I think she's having a bad day."

"I'll say!"

And so Laura and I didn't speak to each other again for the remainder of the day. And now I feel rotten about it. I don't know why I couldn't just keep my big mouth shut. But part of what I said is true. I don't know why she has to act so judgmental and critical sometimes. And in her defense she's not *always* like that. But I also realize her church is fairly conservative and that has to affect her somewhat. But, honestly, sometimes I just wish she would <u>lighten up</u>.

JUDGING NOT

God, what do You think
when we make a stink?
should people go 'round
always putting down
look down their noses
as another mind closes?
o, God, why can't we
be more open and free?
hey, didn't You teach
how it is we'll reach
other ones for You
if we can be true
to the way You live
and how You forgive
with a perfect love
poured from above?
please, help me, I pray
show me Your way

cm